THE NATURE OF THE BEAST

THE NATURE OF THE BEAST

BARBARA V EVERS

Cameleopard Press, Greer, SC

Book Cover created by GetCovers.com

Print ISBN 978-1-959859-18-5
Ebook ISBN 978-1-959859-19-2
First Printing, 2025

*For my high school English teacher, Mary Seamon,
whose words of encouragement to a seventeen-year-old
would-be writer kept me believing someday I'd be published.*

Author's Note

Over the years, I've written and published a variety of short stories. My first collection, *Pieces of Her: Being a Woman is Not For the Faint of Heart*, is a compilation of stories about women dealing with a variety of trials in their lives. This second collection, *The Nature of the Beast*, looks into the heart of the beast in fantasy. You'll find some fantasy, horror, dystopian, time travel, and two stories based on real life. Can you guess which ones?

Lurking between these pages, you'll meet dragons, shifters, small animals, insects, spiders, and the most terrifying beast of all, humans. What is a beast? According to Webster's Online Free Dictionary, a beast is everything from a four-footed mammal to a lower non-human creature to a contemptible human. Are beasts lower than humans? Not in my definition. I think the definition that fits most is the last one listed by Webster's: something formidably difficult to control or deal with.

Enjoy!

Contents

Author's Note   v

The Return of Raker   1

Amends   33

Even Stephen Heathens   39

Not-A-Nut   49

Whippoorwill Calling   53

A Good Trade   59

Buggers   69

1:28 AM   94

Mistake Number Three   101

Lifelike   109

Kaleidoscope   114

Acknowledgements   127
About the Author   128
Also By Barbara V. Evers   129
Excerpt from The Watchers of Moniah   130

1

The Return of Raker

Raker lumbered through the meandering passages of the Grottas Mine, staying clear of Albert's Pass. Even in dragon form, he knew to avoid the popular hangout of the rebellious youth from the hamlet of Sarkany.

Smoke curled from his large nostrils as he snorted over his old-world language—hamlet. Sarkany deserved the label, or it did a hundred years ago, but no matter how hard he tried not to, his thoughts used the ancient languages when he walked as a dragon.

His purple scales scraped along the tight walls heading into the cave. He paused to rub back and forth along an outcropping, a low rumble of pleasure rolling up his throat. With a full belly, he saw no reason not to take advantage of the natural formations leading into his lair. That spot on his left shoulder always itched by the end of a hunting trip. He'd ignored the itch earlier. Easier to ignore tonight. Not so much the unexpected strong call to his soul, begging him to fly over Albert's Pass.

He paused mid-scratch, lifting his snout. The smell of burning wood drifted along the ceiling of the passage. The sweet scent of lilies intertwined with the smoke, tickling his nose.

Her.

With a thunderous bellow, he rushed into his lair. "How did you find me, woman?"

Brigit raised a blue-green stare toward him as he plunged into the large chamber. She sat on a golden, life-sized horse statue near the center of his massive hoard. Her brightly colored peasant skirt dipped into the accumulated treasures heaped throughout the space. The gemstones at her feet reflected their colors in her clear gaze. For a moment, it took him back to the day he first pecked free of his shell, greeted by a much younger version of those eyes—curious, gleeful, and focused.

At the moment, her glare measured him while her mass of red hair bristled around her face in a fiery haze. A warning of what was to come.

With slow, deliberate movements, she slid from the horse and picked her way toward him. "Greetings, Raker."

Scaly tail slamming against the far wall, Raker lunged closer, towering over Brigit. "Why are you here?" His gravelly voice echoed off the walls, but she didn't even blink in response.

"Honestly, Raker." Her no-nonsense, controlled voice did not echo. "It wasn't that hard to find you." Tone shifting to a sharp reprimand, she took a step closer. "Why are *you* here? The Sons of George don't forget, no matter how many years and generations have passed."

The Sons of George. He'd managed to evade them so far, those single-minded raiders. He hadn't anticipated their return to Sarkany, too.

Her slap to his snout came as a shock—she always managed to inflict pain even when he outweighed her several times over. He reared up, mouth open, fire building in his belly.

"Don't you dare." Brigit jabbed a finger at him. "You will not toast me, today. Now change. I can't talk to you when you're like this." Arms crossed, she leveled a scowl at him.

He hunched his shoulders in defiance. She never understood the call that drew him to places he shouldn't go. This time, he'd thought he'd evaded her, but, somehow, she always found him, the she-devil. This time, she wouldn't stop him, though. Not today.

He pushed by her, his tail slapping the mountain of his possessions into a tumbling, clanking rush of jewels, and thundered toward the mine shaft at the other end of the chamber.

Wings folded down his back, he dove into the pit, the thrill of the plunge heating his blood. As he soared toward the bottom of the tunnel, a sudden weight slammed into his back. Pain blasted across his shoulders as Brigit's sharp nails found the spot between his neck scales and dug in. He roared in agony and frustration.

Losing control of the dive, he slammed into the ground with a thud. Staggering to his feet, he shook off the impact and bucked to throw her off his back.

She leapt free, a well-practiced move, but not before jabbing the spot on his neck again.

Unable to resist her pin-pointed attack, Raker hunched over and forced himself to relax into the shift. It hurt more when he fought it, and his sister knew this.

His dragon form folded in on itself. Gas erupted from his lung bladders, fogging the air with sulfur, and his elastic skin contracted, drawing up and forcing him to straighten from his hunched stance. The urge to howl in pain clawed at his mind, but he refused to give her that satisfaction. Bones thickened and shortened. Purple scales melted and fused into smooth golden skin. After several agonizing minutes, Raker stood naked before her, his long, dark hair falling into his face.

Not missing a beat, Brigit advanced on him. "Why Sarkany? Have you found the One?"

"The ancestors lived here." Shoving his hair out of his face, his fingers sought the spot on his neck, the invisible place only she knew how to reach. "They've returned. I smell her."

Brigit tilted her head to the left, studying him. In the darkness of the mine shaft, her eyes glowed with the gift of night vision. Green and sparking with fire, they closed to tiny slits. She shook her head. "You're an idiot."

Fists clenched, Raker bunched his shoulders and took a menacing step toward her, trying to intimidate with his display of great power and size. Not as threatening as the dragon, but still formidable.

She raised an eyebrow at his threat. "Don't be stupid. It's too risky. There are far better places to look."

"Don't you think I have? No matter where I go, I'm drawn here. I can't fight it."

"You're as bad as Cole." The glow in her eyes dimmed for a moment. Her voice lost some of the fire. "Don't let them do this to you, too. To us."

None of her words surprised him. From the day he and Cole pecked free of those hard shells, she'd been there, an excited child ready to care for and protect her brothers under their mother's tutelage. But she'd never been a dragon. She didn't understand. He couldn't let her stop him now. It felt like his last chance. After a few hundred years, one trusted intuition.

Unable to explain, he unleashed the beast, the heat of his change filling the shaft and revealing a myriad of small passages intersecting the dark space. Those passages led him to choose the cavern above as his lair—easy in, easy out when escape became necessary.

"Raker." Brigit's screech echoed from the bottom of the shaft as he shot upward, flames of freedom shooting from his mouth to light the way.

* * *

By mid-morning, Brigit stumbled out of the maze of the Grottas Mine, blinking at the sun. She hadn't spent two-hundred-and-forty-seven years as her brothers' keeper without gaining a few survival skills. Raker might be the last living dragon—all the more reason to take her role seriously. The horizon gave no hints to the dragon's whereabouts. Morning sunlight glittered off the rooftops of Sarkany in the distance.

She slapped at the dirt clinging to her clothes and examined a large rip. "Another skirt ruined thanks to that no-good lizard."

Her gaze returned to the town in the valley. Raker said he smelled the One. To town, then. Hopefully, she wasn't too late to save his scaley, purple hide.

She hiked to where she'd hidden her fully loaded Ford F150 in the small, wooded area below the entrance to the mine. A black vehicle might not have been the best choice for the dry heat of the western US, especially when she needed to blend in, but her heart swelled in pride as it came into sight. A fine film of dirt covered it, just like any other vehicle within a hundred-mile radius.

She dragged a duffel bag from the passenger seat, unwilling to climb into the baked interior of the cab. The water bottles in the bag provided lukewarm refreshment, but she didn't care and stripped down, pouring water over her sweaty body. Wet, red hair twisted into a knot and concealed under a wide-brimmed, leather hat, she donned jeans and a loose-flowing green cotton top. Then the dragon keeper climbed into the truck's cab.

The engine roared to life as she squinted toward the town below. "Maybe the Sons of George won't be looking for Brigit the Brash, yet."

She backed out of the trees and bounced the truck over the rough terrain until she hit the dirt road that led to the main highway. With the windows down, just enough breeze circulated the stuffy air. As the road fed into the highway, she swung a right and headed into Sarkany. Turning up the AC, she powered the windows closed and cranked the Hits from the 70s Sirius station louder, belting out the words to "Carry On My Wayward Son."

A few miles down the highway, which was more of a cracked road with grass and weeds pushing forth to overtake civilization, Brigit passed a young girl walking along the side. Petite with long, dark hair, she looked no more than twelve and offered a friendly wave as Brigit drove by.

Easing off the gas, she studied the girl in the rearview mirror. She wore jeans and a red T-shirt, a pair of sandals dangling from her fingertips. "What's a child doing out here all alone?"

Brigit backed up on the deserted highway until she came abreast of the girl. She lowered her window. "Need a lift?"

A bright smile shone up at her, and Brigit blinked at the unexpected sight. The girl's eyes and golden skin suggested Asian ancestry. Sarkany really had changed since the last time she'd been here. Back then, the town overflowed with Norwegians—the ancestors Raker sought. Easy enough for Raker and Cole to blend in with their sleek and muscular bodies and thick, flowing hair, Raker's dark and Cole's light to match his golden scales. Even she went unremarked with her mass of red hair. They'd found peace there for a time, until the boys stirred the town's dust too much, drawing down the wrath of the Georges. The place hadn't been much more than an outpost back then, but even in tiny settlements, you didn't stay where you weren't welcome. That went triple for dragons.

The girl still smiled at her but hadn't moved to get in.

That brought a sigh of frustration mixed with relief from Brigit. Young though she may be, at least the girl had learned some precautions, even if it did make Brigit's decision to protect her more difficult. Not to mention delay her in locating her brother.

The truck idled. No way was she going to leave this girl in the middle of nowhere. Who knew what monster might come along and snap her up. Brigit was still working out what to say to gain the girl's trust when, with a quick bob of her head, the girl grabbed the door handle and pulled it open. "You know what? I guess it will be all right. The road's hot." She climbed into the truck. "Thanks. I tried to walk in the grass, but there isn't much."

Nodding at the girl's sandals, Brigit asked, "Why not put those on?"

To demonstrate, the girl lifted one and pulled on the strap. Broken.

"Ah. Where ya headed?"

"Only one place this road goes." The girl's rich voice flowed smooth as honey.

Brigit put the truck in gear and started down the road. "It's none of my business, but what are you doing way out here alone?"

The girl shrugged. "The kids from town took me to Albert's Pass."

"And?" Brigit re-evaluated the girl's age. Albert's Pass was teen territory.

"They left me. Some new kid initiation." The girl rolled down the window, her black hair flying in the breeze.

"Kind of young for that group, aren't ya?"

Dimples dotted the child's cheeks. "I'm almost eighteen, just small for my age."

Peeking at her passenger again, Brigit noted the slight curves under the T-shirt hinting at a petite woman. "How long you been out here?"

The girl squinted into the sun, her mouth twisted in thought. "I'm not sure. They took my phone. What time is it?"

Brigit nodded at the clock on the dashboard. "10:48."

"Hm, felt longer. I've been out here almost eleven hours."

The only thing Brigit could do was stare at the girl with concern.

"I know, I know." The girl shrugged. "They picked me up just before midnight, drove us up to the pass, and everyone sat around getting drunk and acting stupid. Anyway, it's what you've got to do to fit in around here. Especially when you arrive near the end of your senior year."

Shaking her head, Brigit took a swallow from a water bottle, then fished her free hand into the duffel bag, pulling out another bottle. She handed it to the girl. "So they left you?"

"Thanks." She accepted the bottle and unscrewed the cap, then took several long gulps. "Not before making me listen to a bunch of stupid stories about dragons and monsters in the hills, then they put out the fire, took my phone, and left me there."

Not good for Raker if the stories still made the rounds. The sooner she found him and got him out of here, the better.

Of all places, why did he choose to return here? His dragon sense would lead him to the One, no matter how far away. They were getting harder to find, though. Last time she'd spoken to him, he'd been headed to Romania. But the women of Sarkany? It may be the boonies but finding a virgin in her mid-twenties had become much harder no matter where you went in the world.

Much less a blond, which he seemed to prefer. Blonds abounded, of course, but virginity was another problem all together. No problem in the ancient days. For a moment, she wished for those simpler times.

But only for a moment. She loved her truck, AC, the ability to get places faster. Maybe Raker was right. Small town values might yield a candidate for the One. Maybe.

"I'm Jade." The girl interrupted Brigit's thoughts. "What's your name? My Uncle Albert will have a fit if I don't know who gave me a ride."

Brigit sputtered, fighting not to choke on the mouthful of water she'd just taken. She coughed, then cleared her throat. "Uncle Albert? As in Albert George?" What fate led the niece of the Sons of George's leader to her on the day Raker sensed the One?

"You know him?" Jade wrinkled her nose in surprise. It made her look even younger.

"Of him." Brigit glanced at the girl, not wanting to be indelicate. "But you're—"

"Not a big strapping Viking?" Jade laughed. "I'm adopted. From China."

"So your name's Jade George?"

"No! That would be awful. Jade Marshall. My mom's Pearl, Albert's sister."

Chewing on this tidbit of unexpected news, Brigit drove the last few miles in silence, not even noticing what songs her favorite station played.

Jade followed her lead for silence until the truck rattled into town. "Just drop me off at the square by the dragon fountain." She shook her head in amusement. "This town and their stories. They say my great-great granddaddy killed the last dragon. That's supposed to be him in the statue."

"I'd heard." Brigit studied the monstrous image of the Viking, a pitchfork shoved into what must be Raker's gaping maw. He almost didn't survive that attack. Their brother, Cole, hadn't, but somehow, she'd managed to heal Raker.

Brigit pulled to a stop in front of the fountain, her gaze fixated on the statues.

"Thanks for the ride and water." Jade climbed out of the truck.

On the other side of the fountain, Albert George stepped out of the local gas station and squinted in their direction. Brigit gripped the wheel, her knuckles turning white. He was older than the pictures she'd located online, hair graying around the temples, but still as burly and menacing as ever.

Oblivious to the potential drama playing out around her, Jade slammed the truck door and walked past the fountain. Her feet slowed as she spotted her uncle's attention riveted on her. Who wouldn't falter under that glare? He said something to her, pointing toward the fountain and Brigit's truck beyond it. Jade shrugged and headed past him.

With a frown, Albert studied the truck, his hand shading his eyes.

On the street corner behind the dragon hunter, Brigit found her brother. Raker lurked, frozen in motion, hungry eyes tracking Jade.

* * *

Raker had spent all morning circling the town at a height that shrank his size to a bird's if anyone bothered to look. Even that high up, the scent of jasmine teased him, begging him to fly closer and closer, but he'd maintained the safety of distance.

The town had mushroomed across the dry land in a hundred years. His enhanced animal sight spotted people moving about their daily chores. Enough that, if he shifted back to human, he might be able to enter the town unnoticed. A cluster of abandoned buildings on the south end of town, the old part he recalled, provided the best location to shift and blend in. He swooped down to land behind a few hills about a mile from there.

Walking on two legs, the tantalizing pull on his dragon senses eased a bit. Relief flooded through him like clouds covering the sun on a hot day. At least he'd remembered to snag his clothing stash during his cave exit. A man might go unnoticed, but not a naked one.

The alluring scent flitted on the breeze, spare though it may be, less noticeable at ground level. *Had she left?* Maybe he'd missed her. Just after midnight last night, his dragon had homed in on the One's location somewhere on the edge of the desert. It had urged him to take up pursuit, but hunger had won that battle. As he wandered the back streets, inhaling the enticing aroma, but unable to fasten onto her location, he kicked himself for giving in to last night's belly grumblings. She was here. His dragon knew it and rumbled in the back of his mind with impatience.

A sudden gust of wind threw the jasmine aroma in his face, drenching him with her scent, and driving him into pursuit. He picked up his stride without thinking about it. The center of town held the prize. She called to his dragon from there.

As he rounded a corner and entered the square, the smooth thrumming of a powerful engine rumbled from the opposite side, drawing closer. His sister's truck came into view moments later. She pulled up to the fountain, easing to a slow stop.

How did the statue look to her? It meant nothing to him anymore, after flying over it in the dark several times. In daylight, the inaccuracies made him smirk. The old George's pitchfork never made it down his throat. It skittered off his teeth when he'd turned and clawed at his family's nemesis. The sculptor created the dragon sitting on his rear haunches, too. Ridiculous, but no one asked him to pose, either.

He snorted, a hint of smoke curling from one nostril. This telltale hint of his nature at least never gave him away. People just assumed he was a smoker. And he was. Just not what they thought.

Voices floated to him on the breeze. The truck's passenger door popped open, and a child hopped out. Not twenty feet away, Albert George stalked out of his station and glared toward Brigit's truck.

Raker shifted his stance, ready to defend his sister.

Funny how she fussed at him about stupidity, and here she was, face to face with only a windshield and short distance between her and their sworn enemy.

A fresh wave of jasmine flooded his sinuses, and he stumbled at the intensity of the fragrance. The child who had climbed out of the truck paused in front of Albert and said something, then the most thrilling ripple of laughter transformed her face as she walked past the older man. Raker leaned toward it, taking in her grace and beauty, the smooth way she walked and the slight swing of her hips.

She was too young. Had it been so long his dragon didn't know better? He stood frozen to the spot as she approached the gas pumps. His gaze swept over her, taking in the curves of a woman, the smile of self-confidence. Not a child, after all, but still too young. He took a step, the weight of indecision warring with the involuntary motion. Another step. Then another.

Deep brown eyes flashed toward him in surprise, but she greeted him with a welcoming grin. His heart thumped as loud as the dragon's as he eased toward her.

"Hello?" Her voice, rich and melodious, wound around his throat like a bewitching snake.

"Hello," he managed to croak out.

She glanced around. "Did you need something?"

Yes. You.

Instead, he reached out to smooth a wayward strand of hair from her face.

She jerked back, eyes widening.

"Sorry," Raker said. "You have something caught in your hair."

"Oh." She smiled, a flush rising in her cheeks. "You startled me." She tilted her head, trying to find it. "Where?"

"Let me." This time she remained still, her gaze caught on his as he plucked a tiny blade of grass from the strand of glossy black hair and smoothed the hair from her face. It felt like silk gliding across his hand. His fingers brushed her cheek, warm and damp with perspiration. Not sweat. Never sweat for someone so perfect.

The rev of an engine drew his gaze back to the fountain. His sister's truck screeched past the statue and headed straight for him. Dust stirred the quiet air, and the girl spun around in surprise.

The truck jerked to a halt, Brigit's green eyes transformed to frigid blue. "Get in."

One last look at this marvelous creature. "Bye." He yanked the door open and jumped in, risking one last glance before pulling the door closed.

Her palm to the spot where he'd touched her, the girl whispered, "Bye."

* * *

Albert George tried to calm his breathing. The woman in the truck stared at him, body frozen in time. He turned to his niece.

"Jade?" Albert restrained his voice, seeking to conceal the knife edge of worry. "It's not safe for you to be out here alone."

The girl paused and tilted her head in confusion. "I wasn't."

A strange tingle ran along Albert's spine just like his father and grandfather told him it would. Could it be? Didn't he have four more years to prepare? He sniffed the air, gagging on the slight hint of sulfur. The woman in the truck still stared back at him. He jutted his chin in her direction. "Who's that?"

Jade turned and squinted back at the driver, surprise flashing over her face. "Um, I asked, but...I don't think she said." She shrugged one shoulder. "She knows you. She's not familiar?"

"Didn't say that," he growled.

The child's flippant attitude scratched all over his nerves. His sister had kept her away too long. She'd never learn, and if the driver of that truck was who he suspected she was, Jade's training just jumped to critical.

He took one step toward Jade, towering over her slight form, and pointed at the fountain. "That wasn't the last dragon."

Jade laughed out loud. "Yeah, right. You're as crazy as the rest of the hicks in this town." She shook her head and ambled toward the gas station, laughter trailing behind her like an overpowering perfume.

The truck still idled by the fountain. Albert strode toward it with determination. His heart thrummed in his chest, excitement twisting through his worry. All his life, he'd waited for the chance to earn the leader title he'd inherited. A dragon—part of his nightmares and his hopes and dreams. Could the driver be Brigit? He got within a few yards of the truck, and the woman startled like a surprised bird, revved the engine, and burned rubber only to screech to a stop by the gas pumps.

Dust and grit flew up in her trail, making him blink a few times before he could see clearly. Jade stood beside the pumps. A dark-haired man hovered over her, his body leaning in close and possessive. The man stroked her cheek once.

Albert's stomach churned at the sight, and he raced to intercept the man. "Jade! Get away from him!"

The dark man glanced at Albert, said something, then leapt into the woman's waiting truck. It sped away kicking up a cloud to match the windstorm that blew through last week.

Albert skidded to a stop next to Jade. "Did he hurt you? What did he say?"

His niece turned sparkling eyes his way. A secret smile spread over her face. "What?"

Patience, his sister had urged. Well, patience be damned. He didn't have time for silly girls to get caught up in a dragon's maze of treachery and temptation. It never ended well. He grabbed her by the arm and dragged her toward the store, through the entrance, and all the way to his office in the back, ignoring the startled stares of the clerk and few customers.

"Sit." He pointed at a plain, industrial metal chair with a faded black vinyl cushion. A rip in the fabric spilled yellowed foam rubber.

She obeyed, although he didn't miss the roll of her eyes and the defiance in her posture as she slumped down, arms crossed over her chest.

Ignoring the rebellious teen act, he turned to the old safe behind his desk. It stood almost as tall as he, and the faded black metal exterior showed its age in dings and scratches. He spun the dial three times, cranked the wheel, and the door swung open. With steady hands, he hauled out the large leather case containing his spear gun and crossbow and slammed it on his desk with a thud. The sight and feel of them eased his nerves.

"I should've smelled him sooner." He strapped on his holster. "Were you with him last night? It didn't escape my notice you didn't spend the night in your bed."

Alarm popped on Jade's face for a mere second before she squashed it down and regarded him with a façade of indifference. "No."

Any other day, he might have laughed at this. His own sister had the same control on her reactions. Nature versus nurture had one answer, now.

"Then where were you?"

She shrugged and refused to make eye contact.

"There's a lot you don't understand." He jabbed at a faded yellow WANTED poster on the wall. "Is this the woman in the truck?"

Not for the first time, he wished the poster of the dragon man had survived. He hadn't gotten a good look at the man in the square, but if Brigit drove that truck, then...He ground his teeth together waiting Jade's silence out.

She rubbed her hands along her arms. Why the teens today refused to dress with modesty, he didn't understand. At least her size suggested a much younger girl, so most boys left her alone. Unless they knew her. But a dragon? He'd be drawn to her. Albert's skin crawled as he thought of that man touching Jade. And she'd let him. This same girl who rebuffed every Tom, Dick, and Harry who came sniffing around from the local high school since she'd arrived.

When she still didn't answer, he turned his parental disapproving stare on her. "Answer me. Is that the woman?"

She sneered. "That's like from the old west or something."

He reached for his knife holster and strapped it on. "Doesn't matter. Is that her?"

When she still didn't respond, he yanked the poster off the wall and shoved it in her face. "Take a good look. Is it her?"

"Uncle, you're scaring me. Do you want me to call Mama? You having a fit or something?"

"No. Your mother's made this hard enough, keeping you away all these years." He ran a hand through his hair and tried to soften his voice. "Just look at the picture. Does it look like her?"

She shook her head. "It can't be."

Her refusal to say yes or no told him what he already knew. He yanked the receiver off his desk phone and jabbed the red button, the one he'd longed to punch all his life. Eyes on Jade, he held the phone to his ear. When his brother's voice answered, he barked out the words. "Potential sighting. Assemble the Sons."

Those beautiful, dark eyes looked up at him when he hung up the phone, confusion erasing her negativity for a moment. "Is it her grandmother?"

Albert grabbed the case from his desk and shoved past Jade. "This wasn't supposed to happen yet. We thought I'd have four summers to train you. Four more after that hunting him."

"Four? Four more?" Jade's voice jumped an octave as she leapt out of the seat. "Here? No thanks."

"Jade." He paused in the doorway, swarming with guilt over the jolt of shock he needed to deliver but couldn't. Not if he was going to stop that dragon. "You're here for a reason. My sister adopted you on purpose."

"I know that. She's told me how she wanted a child. And then she found me."

He relaxed his stance and faced her, trying not to look so ominous. "We all love you." He placed his free hand on her shoulder. "It took a lot of historical research to find you. It *had* to be you."

His niece backed up against the wall, looking young, small, and afraid. "I don't understand."

Every nerve in his body told him not to say it, but how much longer could he keep her in the dark? The dragon had found her. He'd touched her. She had to understand.

Stepping back into the room, he eased the door closed. Took only one more step, not wanting to spook Jade more. "Your grandmother's ancestors honored the dragons of old. The women..." He hesitated, unwilling to disclose the role her ancestors played. Slinging the bag over his shoulder, he about-faced and yanked the door open. "Go to your mother. Tell her what's happened. Tell her I said she needs to tell you."

Albert marched out of the office. Eighteen was too young to learn you're dragon bait.

* * *

Jade stared after her uncle, stomach churning with fear. Her ancestors? The man was crazy. The whole town just like him. She stormed out of the office and rushed toward the store's exit. Through the front windows, she saw her uncles and cousins gathering in the street. Three pick-up trucks bristled with men armed like her uncle. The throaty thrum of several Harleys turned her attention to the left. Albert and three of their many relatives straddled motorcycles. With a wave of his hand, Albert pulled out and the rest fell in behind him.

People on the street paused to watch the armed caravan, then turned back to their everyday concerns as if this happened every day.

"Whoo-ee." An older man's voice sounded behind her. "Looks like we got us a dragon hunt."

She turned to stare at the man, and he grinned at her, teeth brown and crooked. "Now don't you worry none, little girl. The Georges will keep us safe." Cackling, he shuffled out the door.

The heat of the day did nothing to quell the cold chills running down Jade's arms as she rushed out of the store and headed for the small house in Uncle Albert's backyard. The street they lived on looked calm, normal, if a little bare of color like the rest of this town. She pushed through the front door, calling out. "Mom?"

From the back room, she heard the crackle of a staticky voice and followed it.

"Mom?"

Pearl Marshall looked up, hand hesitating on one of the black dials of the weird machine Jade had asked about when they moved in. A ham radio, her dad told her.

Wrinkles furrowed her mother's fair brow, her hair tumbling over her face in disarray. The fingers of her mother's hand shook as she adjusted the dial. "Hush. I'm trying to listen."

Over the crackle, Albert's voice fought against the static. It sounded like when she hit a no cell signal spot with her phone.

"What—"

"Shh." Her mother flapped a hand at her. "I can't hear." Grabbing a huge headset, she fumbled with the cord and jabbed it in the headphone socket of the radio then shoved the headset over her ears. She closed her eyes and listened.

Jade sagged in frustration and turned to leave. A strong hand seized her wrist and held her in place. She turned to meet her mother's familiar blue eyes, widened in fright—a look not so familiar.

Seconds later, her mother popped up, throwing the headset on the desk. "We've got to go. Run. Pack. Only what you need. Enough for a few days. Leave the rest. We don't have time."

"Go? Why—"

"I said now. Don't ask questions." She dragged a duffle bag out from under the bed.

When Jade remained standing there, her mother shoved past her, yanked open drawers, and grabbed handfuls of clothing. She stuffed them into the bag, opened a drawer in the bedside table, and pulled out a gun.

"Where did you get that?"

"Never mind." She shoved it in her waistband. "Go. Pack."

Had everyone lost their minds in this town? Maybe it was a good thing to leave. She hated it here, anyway. Jade rushed to her room, pulled out her big suitcase, and opened her drawers. What should she take? Mom said a few days' worth.

"Not that suitcase. Too big." Her mother rushed into the room, tossed the large suitcase off the bed, and turned to fling the closet door open. "Use this one." She pulled a hiking backpack off the closet floor. "If it doesn't fit in here, you don't need it."

"Nothing will fit in there."

Exasperation, tinged with fury, crossed her mother's face. "Fine. Move." She nudged Jade out of the way. "I'll do it."

No more than five minutes later, her mother hustled them out the door to the Jeep in the backyard. She tossed her bag behind the seat and jumped in. The engine roared to life and her mother looked up at Jade. "Get in."

"But Mama. What's happening?" Jade fought a sudden urge to cry; her lip trembled.

The tension in her mother's body drained away. She climbed out of the Jeep and walked around to her daughter, enveloping her in a consoling hug. "Oh honey. I know this is frightening. Just trust me. Please?"

Sniffling, Jade nodded, drawing comfort from her mother's arms.

"Good." Pearl chucked her under the chin. "Get in. I'll tell you what I can."

The Jeep jerked when her mother put it in gear and floored it. Jade clung to the seat, praying to wake up.

* * *

Brigit took her frustration out on the F-150's gas pedal. "What were you thinking?"

Over the roar of the engine and rush of the wind through the windows, Raker shouted, "You really have to ask?"

The truck fishtailed down the highway heading into the desert. As she bounced over potholes, she prayed for protection, speed, and the undercarriage of her truck. Sure, she could replace the truck. Not Raker though. Guilt settled over her jangled nerves one more time. It sounded like the right thing to do five years ago. Split up. Search the world for the One. Time was running out.

Faces and dragons flashed through her memory. Their mother bending to kiss her good night, the three eggs tucked warmly by her bed. "They're your responsibility Brigit. You live so dragons may live. Don't let us down."

She had tried.

They'd lost their father and mother and two brothers, one who never made it to his first shift, Raker's egg mate. Always her favorite, Raker needed to survive his dragon's confused libido. The alternative? If he died without offspring, she'd—. She stomped the accelerator.

Brigit spun the wheel, tires screeching as they bounced off the highway and veered onto a dirt road leading into the desert. If she didn't say anything soon, she might explode. "She's only eighteen, Raker. And Albert George's niece. Nice choice."

Silence greeted that news, and Brigit slowed the truck as she glanced at her charge. The desolation on his face drew her back a hundred years. A high wall of flames licked the sky over Sarkany that day. From the look of things, parts of the small town never fully recovered.

Neither had Raker.

The destruction her brothers had wrought on the place saddened her. It didn't have to be this way. There'd been a time when people flocked to the dragons, young daughters in tow, each family hopeful for the honor and treasure that came with becoming the One. At least, that's what her mother told her. Their mother should know. She'd been one of those daughters. The last of a dying breed.

Civilization didn't believe in legends anymore, except for the Sons of George. Why had that family multiplied while hers dwindled to two?

She stopped at the crest of a hill, the truck turned to face toward Sarkany. Below, a small cloud of dust billowed behind three trucks and four motorcycles heading toward them. The Sons of George wasted no time in pursuit.

Raker scrubbed at his face and groaned. "I don't know why I smelled her so early. I knew she was too young the moment I saw her, but," he shook his head, "I couldn't stop the dragon."

The dust cloud drew closer.

Fear and compassion shot metallic adrenaline into Brigit's soul. The surge embittered her voice. "Get out. Change. I'll distract them and seek you later."

"No." He pounded a fist on the dashboard, the light of the dragon burning in his eyes. "I'll protect you."

"Fool." She rounded on him. "You die, I die. Get out."

Motions smooth and graceful, Raker turned to his sister and cupped her cheek in his hand. "We'll manage. We always have." He placed a kiss on her forehead, his lips dry against her sweat, then slid out of the truck. "I'll see you soon."

The shadow of her brother walked away from the truck, the dust from her pell-mell trip swirling around him. Light around him grew, then blossomed into a burst of fire as he shifted. That perfect skin edged into purple scales while she held her breath. God, he was beautiful.

"Live," she whispered and turned the truck around.

* * *

Albert scanned the horizon for signs of the dragon. They'd lost the truck, amid the swirling dust, but could still follow its tracks.

His grandpa had warned him not to dream of this day. "Best hope you never see one, my boy," he'd rasped while he rocked on the porch, the stump of a pipe clenched between his teeth. "Them's awful mean and hard to kill."

Nine at the time, he'd tried to study the slash of scars running down the old man's face from his black eye patch, down his neck, and into his shirt collar.

Catching Albert's look, the old man leaned over and lifted the patch. "Take a good look boy. This is what happens if you get close enough to kill one."

The skin was puckered and tight like someone took the lids and sewed them together in an uneven line. A sudden desire to touch the seam overwhelmed him, and he gripped his fists together to stop the notion.

His grandfather may have been one-eyed, but he didn't miss much. "Touch it. Go on. It won't bite."

He extended one finger but couldn't bring himself to get close enough. With a warrior's grip, the old patriarch yanked his finger toward the spot and ran it back and forth over the ripple of flesh. "Never had a chance at a fake eyeball, ya know. A dragon's scratch carries many diseases. My 'ole face blew up like a red balloon for days."

The man's hacking laugh had followed Albert as he yanked his finger back and scurried off the front porch to the cool welcome of the grass on his bare feet.

Albert trembled over the memory while his Harley ate up the road. The old man and his predecessors rode horses, expensive breeds, to chase dragons. The Harley still wasn't fast enough. His niece. They suspected, no, counted on her ancestry, but the accuracy of his sister's research still tasted bitter on his tongue.

"There." The shout came from his cousin, Edwin, as he peered through binoculars from the back of the pickup closest to Albert.

A great shadow rose above a hill a few miles to their west, wings flapping in large cumbersome arcs as the beast ascended into the sky.

Albert stared, his hand letting up on the throttle. Around him, the others slowed, too, awe and fear flashing in their faces. That thing. That dragon wheeled in the sky and turned toward them. It soared in their direction faster than anything that size should move. The shadow plunged from above, screeching like the wind whistling through a tunnel during a sandstorm. The great body blocked out the sun, casting a cool shadow for a moment.

Albert's mind snapped back into awareness. The cool shadow lulled prey until it was too late. "Duck."

The dragon's maw released a blast of fire as the men dove for the ground. Two of the trucks burst into flame as the beast wheeled around for another attack. The roar of fire crackled in his ears as Albert scrambled for his crossbow, sighting for the dragon's heart.

A haze of sulfur fogged over him, and he coughed.

His brother, Robert, stepped up beside him, crossbow armed and ready. The two turned together and braced for the next dive. The dragon arced upward, out of reach, and the two men glanced at each other.

"Ho-oly!" Robert's grin didn't hide the tremor in his voice.

The whomp of leathery wings drew their attention back to the awful sight. The behemoth dove toward them, and they both re-leased. One bolt bounced off the hard scales. One tore a jagged hole in the dragon's left wing. An ungodly screech shattered their ears.

The dragon wheeled around and retreated toward the hills. With two huge flaps, it covered the distance to the first of the hills and dove out of view.

Albert and Robert leapt on their fallen bikes and raced after the fleeing dragon. Behind them, a concussive explosion threw waves of heat across the land. Albert ducked by reflex and prayed they'd made it far enough to escape the fate of those in the trucks. Those inside, brothers in the Sons of George, were gone the moment the dragon spewed his rage at them. An honorable death.

It took forever to reach that first hill. When Albert crested it, the dragon had disappeared. In the distance, dust trailed Brigit the Brash's truck. Albert gunned his engine, but the truck and dragon were too far away.

* * *

Brigit kept one eye on the dirt track she roared down while she watched her brother disappear over the distant mountains. Déjà vu hit her hard. Except this time, she rode eight times more horsepower than their pursuers. She couldn't see him yet, but Albert George was back there. Hopefully, he'd give up soon.

A thick cloud of smoke rose from the direction Raker had come from. She bit her lip. Fire created a distraction unless he'd injured or killed one of the Sons. A chill ran over her.

From the short exposure she'd had to Albert George, she could see he'd inherited his grandsire's stubborn determination. If Raker had hurt anyone, he'd given the Sons of George enough cause to never stop hunting him. And her.

A flash of reflected sunlight in the rearview mirror rocketed an electric current of adrenaline along her nerves. Two motorcycles roared down the first hill in pursuit. A mile or two back, but they followed her tracks.

She hit the gas and swung left, leading them on a wild dragon chase away from her brother.

* * *

After several minutes of frantic driving, crisscrossing back and forth over her tracks, Brigit eased the truck to a halt. She turned off the engine and listened for sounds of pursuit. Except for the hot engine's ticking, silence greeted her. With relief, she slumped backward in her seat, heaving a huge sigh.

Then her gaze fell on the empty water bottle in the passenger door. Jade's. What had happened to the girl? She obviously didn't know the part she played in this feud. For that matter, what part did she play? Why would the Georges adopt a child from China?

Icy claws of fear skittered up her arms as she considered this. Romanians honored dragons, true, but they'd turned their backs on the old ways. Many of the Chinese hadn't. Had the Georges chosen the child of an ancient family to draw Raker out? What kind of sick, demented family would do that?

Of course, what kind of sick, demented dragon would go after the One too soon?

A desperate one.

"Now what?" Exhausted more than she'd been in a hundred years, Brigit leaned her head back and closed her eyes. Raker couldn't mate with Jade.

Not yet.

Not ever.

Too risky.

He must find a true One—a woman, not an almost woman.

As for Jade, would the Georges explain it to her? This morning, the girl laughed at the idea of dragons. She didn't know the truth. Now?

Putting the truck in gear, Brigit headed back toward Raker's lair, praying he'd fled there and waited for her return. They would set the charges prepared in advance to collapse the cavern's entry and protect his treasure—a safeguard of all dragon kind—and get their tails out of Dodge.

* * *

As the Jeep bumped along the highway, Jade waited for her mother to say something. At the moment, the frown and wrinkles creasing her mother's high forehead screamed at Jade to wait.

Waiting. She'd never been good at that. Except where boys were concerned. None of them intrigued her.

She felt the touch of the quiet man in the street this morning and traced her fingers over the spot. *He* intrigued her. Funny, she couldn't recall his face. He'd disappeared into that truck so fast. The same truck that brought her to town. Did he know that woman?

Forgetting her resolve to not disturb her mother, she blurted out, "Who's Brigit the Brash?"

The startled look her mother flashed her way didn't help calm Jade's nerves. What was wrong with her family today? They were acting like the kids last night. Idiots. Superstitious idiots.

"Where did you hear that name?"

"Uncle Albert showed me an old poster. Asked me if I'd seen her."

"He what?" The Jeep jerked to a halt as her mother slammed on the brakes.

"Showed me some old-timey WANTED poster. Had a drawing of Brigit the Brash."

"Why would he think you'd seen her?"

"That's what I asked."

Frown deepening, her mother pressed the gas but drove at a more reasonable speed now. "What did he tell you?"

"Not much. Something about ancestors and to ask you."

"That lying idiot." Her mother slammed her fist into the dashboard.

"Mom!" Pearl Marshall never gave in to violence. Never.

"Sorry. What did he say about ancestors?"

"Nothing much. He was acting crazy, pulling out weapons, waving that poster in my face, telling me he had to train me." She paused. "I'm not staying here for eight years am I?"

"Not anymore."

"Anymore?"

Pearl glanced over at her daughter, her mouth trying to lift in a smile. It didn't succeed, making Jade's stomach churn more.

"Your uncle has ideas. About you. About. . ."

"Don't say dragons."

A sarcastic laugh erupted from her mother's mouth. "Yes. Dragons."

Jade slumped down in the seat, arms crossed. "He's crazy, right?"

Her mother nodded. "In some ways." She patted her daughter's leg. "Don't worry. I won't let him pull you into the family business."

They both jumped as an explosion rocked the ground. Pearl jerked the Jeep onto the shoulder of the road. Screeched to a halt. She spun to look behind them, face turning pale.

Jade turned. A large plume of smoke rose in the sky several miles behind them. "Is that the town?"

"I don't think so. It's farther away." Lip caught between her teeth, her mother sat back and pulled out her phone. She stared at the screen for a few heartbeats but didn't activate it.

"Nope. Not this time, bro. You've dug this pit. Dig out on your own." She repocketed the phone and eased out onto the road again.

Jade bit her tongue. Why had her mother looked at her phone? None of this made sense. She twisted to look behind them. The plume of smoke had grown. She wasn't sure she wanted to know what was going on, after all.

* * *

Raker wasn't in the cavern. Brigit paced the entrance, watching the billowing smoke in the distance. That much fire in the open desert meant he'd destroyed something. Only two motorcycles kept up the chase. Were the rest dead?

Heart pounding, she rushed down the hill. She had to find him before someone dangerous did.

Agonizing minutes later, she pulled back onto the highway and headed for the one place she dreaded—Sarkany. For a long time, the road lay empty. Then she saw him, coasting to a landing off to her right. He dropped toward the ground too fast. His angle odd. Her heart pushed into her throat. Raker prided himself on smooth landings.

Heading cross-country, she bumped the truck along the uneven terrain. By the time she reached him, he'd shifted and sat on the ground, cradling his right arm. Throwing the truck in Park, she flung the door open and hurried to him. Covered in dust, he looked up at her, eyes bleak with sorrow and pain.

"Let me see." She knelt beside him. A long and deep gash ran down his forearm. Contrary to folklore, the shift would not heal him fully, but it did stem the bleeding.

"Sit tight."

Every dragon keeper maintained a large medical kit. She climbed into the truck bed and opened the built-in storage locker. Moments later, she returned with cleanser, sutures, antibiotic ointment, and bandaging.

Starting to clean the wound, she didn't look at him. "You won't be flying for a few weeks."

He nodded, and his body tensed as she poured alcohol over the gash.

After irrigating the wound, she made short work of stitching him up. It didn't take long when you'd done it a thousand times. After applying a good coating of antibiotic and thorough dressing, she rose and held her hand out to him. "Let's go."

Without a word, he followed her to the truck.

"Pants in the glove box."

Raker nodded and popped the door open. This time neither one of them giggled and pointed out a glove wasn't going to help him right now. Maybe next time.

Engine rumbling to life, she turned toward the highway. In the distance, a Jeep headed down the long stretch of highway coming out of town. As it zoomed past, Raker sat up, body tensing and alert. "It's her." He reached for the door.

"No, baby." She laid a gentle hand on his arm. "You can't go after her. Not now." She paused and breathed in and out before adding, "Not ever."

Embers burned in his eyes as he jerked his head up to stare at her.

She said nothing more. Just waited.

Eventually, he nodded, and Brigit found she could breathe again.

"You're right." He raised his head and sniffed the air. "Her scent calls me, though. I could track her easily."

Heart thumping hard and slow at his words, she shook her head. "No, you can't. You need your dragon to do that." She hesitated at the highway. Right toward Sarkany or left toward Jade?

Raker watched her, nodding. "You're right. We need to find the One together—you, me, and the dragon. Where should we go?"

"Home. Romania. We'll search there. She's not old enough to be the One. That means another is out there somewhere."

"Of course." He slumped against the door. "I'm tired."

"Sleep." His hair felt damp as she ran her hand through it. "Sleep."

When he settled into the deep breathing of slumber, she turned left. She'd go slow, find the first crossroad and sniff the air. Raker didn't know she sometimes smelled the odors of the women who drew him. She'd go the opposite way than the Jeep and Jade.

He looked young and helpless curled up on the seat. He'd come so close this time. She wanted to pound the steering wheel and wail her frustrations, but that would only wake him.

Distance and time. That's what he needed to forget Jade. Then they'd continue their quest to find a more suitable One and preserve their kind. Live to fight one more day.

Unless, of course, his desperate dragon heart won the battle and killed them first.

Authors Note: Did you enjoy Jade, Raker, and Brigit?
If so, never fear! I have plans for them. This is their backstory.

2

Amends

"You need to call Steve."

"Who is this?" Chelsea double-checked the caller ID on her phone—Knoxville, Tennessee. Did she know anyone in Knoxville? "I think you have the wrong number." She started to end the call.

The deep, masculine voice rose, as if he knew her finger hovered over the End button. "I know this sounds weird. Please, don't hang up. You *are* Chelsea, aren't you?"

She fought the urge to disobey his plea and failed. "Yes, but—"

"Chelsea Hanson?"

She glanced at the caller's number again. "Who is this?"

There was a pause, then the caller blew out a long breath. "You don't know me. I know, I know. That sounds weird, too, but Steve needs to talk to you. Call him."

Chelsea inhaled at the strength of his command. Outside her window an ink-black crow sat on the deck railing. A few drops of rain fell, big splats on the stained wooden deck. The bird took flight, and she wished she could follow its lead. "Look. I don't know how you got this number, but I have better things to do than play the name game with you. Either give me your name or I hang up."

"If you do, I'll call Joshua, instead."

Heart thudding, she fought down a growl. "You're threatening me?"

He rattled off his response. "No. I'm sorry. I'm John. Look, my name isn't important. You need to call Steve Andingham."

She dropped down, hard, onto the stool beside her.

In a flash, she was there. The last time she saw Steve. In his kitchen. He'd gripped a roasting pan between two mitted hands and stared into her eyes, his puppy-dog gaze wounded. The stench of burnt pot roast filled her nostrils again, and she grabbed her glass of water to wash the memory away.

She always wondered if he'd cried later. Cried when she'd walked out.

"I haven't heard that name in...in five years."

"Well, I've heard your name, Chelsea. Every day for the last six months. I've known Steve for a long time. He never breathed a word about you until May." Another long pause with a deep breath. "He won't stop."

A shiver raised her hackles. He wouldn't stop talking about her? If he fixated on her again, he'd be hard to shake off.

They'd moved on. At least she had.

She glanced at the engagement ring on her hand. She didn't need Steve's chaotic complications. Joshua was everything Steve never could be. Kind, considerate, employed, a good human being. Steve had always complicated things. And here he was, sniffing around where he shouldn't, again.

She ended the call. Tossed her phone on the counter.

It lit up, vibrating with insistence.

She turned away. The crow was back, and she willed it to help her.

The phone stopped buzzing but started up again.

On his fourth call she gave up. "What?"

"Are you there?"

"Yes." She heard the recalcitrant note in her voice, just like one of her middle school students. She couldn't let the jerk take her back there again, to bad attitudes and frightening nights. "I haven't seen him in five years. Get him counseling or something." Could she hang up and reach Joshua first? And say what? "Just stop calling."

"Wait." John's voice barked at her with an urgency she wished she could ignore.

She waited. A drop of rain made a slow angled path down the kitchen window.

"I promise he needs to talk to you."

"Why didn't he call, then?" Now she heard fourteen-year-old scorn in her voice. She needed to put an end to this before she reverted to her students' ages.

"He's not thinking straight."

Annoyance fought with the fear in her chest. She got up from the stool, pacing back and forth in her small kitchen. If he called Joshua . . .

A spot on the counter drew her attention, and she grabbed a damp washrag from the sink and scrubbed at it. "What makes you the expert?"

"He's in recovery, Chelsea. You're the only one he can't get the nerve to call."

How many times had she begged Steve to get help? Find someone to tame the beast inside him?

"Are you there?"

"For some reason, I am." She shoved a hand through her hair. "Look, I'm glad he's in rehab or whatever, but I don't see what it has to do with me."

"You're not familiar with the steps then?"

Twelve if she recalled. One about making amends. The best way he could do that was to leave her alone. "I don't need his apology."

John's voice turned confident. Or was it smug? "I think you will appreciate his amends."

"Ha." Steve couldn't do anything she'd appreciate. "You said he doesn't want to call me. He's fixing his life. That's great. I've moved on. I don't need, no, I don't want to see him or even hear his voice. It's taken a long time to learn to live with what he did to me."

The crow landed on the windowsill and pecked at the screen. She shooed at it, flapping her hand at the window. It paused, tilting its head to study her with one beady eye. then pecked again.

"There's a cure."

That made her stop flapping. A cure? For just him or for her, too? Just the thought drew her gaze to the carpet covering deep scratches on the floor. Joshua would never need to know her dark secret.

"What kind of cure?"

"The only kind you're interested in."

She paced the kitchen faster, like a caged animal. The truth or was this a ploy? Men like Steve didn't give up their women easily, especially to another man. Had he learned about Joshua? A whine threatened in her throat, and she muzzled it to silence.

"What does it take?"

"An injection given during a full moon when you're at your worst."

At her worst? She stared at the concealing rug again. She'd kept her nature leashed and under control for so long, no one knew about her affliction. Not even Joshua. "And who is stupid enough to get close to me then?"

"It has to be Steve."

"No." The word leapt from her lips without thought.

"It has to be the one who infected you, Chelsea. No one else."

The next full moon was in a week. She'd told Joshua she had an out-of-town meeting, so he'd not miss her. Was she really considering this?

"Are you his alpha?"

"Not anymore." The man barked a laugh. "I've already taken the cure."

"And Steve? He's done it, too? It works. He's not . . . you know, anymore?"

"He hasn't shifted in six months. I haven't in nine. It works."

The crow squawked at her. She turned to the window and bared her teeth. In a flurry of wings, it darted away leaving a trail of droppings on the windowsill.

"What's it cost?"

"Nothing. He must pay for what he did. Not you. Unless, of course, you've infected—"

"No. I'm not that stupid."

"Impressive." Was that sarcasm or amusement in his voice? "I'll send you the coordinates and a contract."

Those words skittered her pulse. "Why do you need a contract?"

"We don't. You do. To ensure we do what we say we'll do and leave you alone once you're cured. So will you come?"

"What other choice do I have?" She ended the call and flung the dishrag into the sink. The rain clattered against the window, several more drops rushing after the first ones. Their response to nature taunting her.

With a sigh, she glanced at her phone as the text came through. Coordinates.

The crow perched on the windowsill again, head cocked to study her.

"I guess I'm going on a trip." She rapped on the window, and the crow flew away.

Author's Note: This story has changed a LOT since the first draft. In case you wondered, I don't know why the crow shows up. It just does.

3

Even Stephen Heathens

The early morning sunlight slanted through the red and orange leaves of the trees bordering the marketplace as my brother, Sean, and I approached our family's apple stall. I groaned as I saw the waiting line curving down the cracked-asphalt roadway that ran through the middle of the market. Less than half of the customers would get to buy apples from me today. Hopefully, people would behave.

In the background, I heard the squawks of chickens and other animals, the clang of metal, and the low hum of anxious people waiting. I studied our customers, trying not to make eye contact, checking for troublemakers in the horde. Several large boys, flush with the early years of manhood, held the first spots in the line, dancing back in forth in a punching game of bravado while they waited. A quick check of the other stalls told me what I already knew—boys just like these held the prime spots in every line. Their shouts and laughter mingled with those of children swarming around the young mothers who'd managed to shove into the second-best spots.

No one dared dispute these two groups their positions.

As always, the oldest and frailest had been pushed to the ends of the lines. My former Philosophy teacher, George, stood a little past the halfway point, his back rounded with age, eyes rheumy with cataracts. If only I could bring all our apple crop. I'd give him some of the big goldens just to see his eyes light up as the juice dribbled into his matted beard.

I basked in that dream for a moment, recognizing it for the dangerous fantasy it was. If the Regulators learned our farm produced more apples than we claimed, they'd seize the house and land for the good of the people. What they didn't know wouldn't hurt them, and it kept us safe in the home of my father and his grandfather before him. I suspected the other stall-owners hid their true provenance, too, although no one ever discussed or suggested it.

Inside the six-by-five-foot shack, I lit the small heater. Sean placed our two baskets, measly offerings that they were, on the shelves below the counter. "There you go, Grace. Be careful today." He nodded in the direction of the market. "That mob looks antsy. Do you have your pistol?"

The gun weighed down the hidden pocket in my skirt and could get me thrown in the stocks, but I dared not come to market without it.

After a quick hug, Sean ducked out the rear door. I unlocked the shutters and shoved them open to greet our customers.

The chill kept people moving quickly and, before I knew it, only a few apples rolled around the bottom of the second basket. I glanced around for one of the red-uniformed Regulators who enforced the sales limits and ensured we earned our basic allotments, nothing more. They turned away unlucky patrons when a stall ran out of stock, a necessary evil some of them enjoyed too much.

None of these men in sight. I leaned over the counter, fighting the nerves churning in my belly, and sniffed the cool October air, parsing the stench of unwashed bodies from the crisp scents of a world in full-blown autumn. A hint of anxiety hovered over the market, the odor pungent and hard to explain, but easy to recognize once you've experienced it.

To my right, the line for the herbal woman's stall curled in a coughing, sniffling queue twice as long as mine. To my left. Jerome's corn stall stood empty, his stock sold out a few weeks ago.

"Get on with it, Grace." An older woman, bundled in frayed and faded scarves and a moth-eaten coat, rapped her knuckles on the counter. "I ain't standing out here freezing for nothin'."

I picked up an apple, and she extended her right arm under the laser scanner on the counter, her wrist turned up. The Peacekeeper, a name more ironic than its maker ever knew, beeped approval as it scanned her chip. I handed her the apple which she took a big bite from before hurrying toward another stall.

Five apples left. Philosopher George stood eight people back in the line.

The next two customers received their allotted apples and hurried toward the chicken farmer's stall across the way, giving the herbal woman's line a wide berth. I doubted Benjamin still had eggs to sell, but you took your chances on market day.

A man shuffled up to my counter, cleared his throat, and spat a huge stream of brown tobacco juice on the ground.

"G'morning, Matthias. Did your chip update, yet?" I bit my lip, knowing his answer before he spoke.

He'd tried to buy an apple each of the last two market days, but the Peacekeeper buzzed its denial, declaring a zero balance.

Each of us received the same allotment once a week. Enough to live on according to the lawmakers, but the law didn't tell us how to spend it. Every village had a Matthias or two.

His spindly arm shot out from his overlong coat sleeve. He grabbed my right arm with surprising strength. "Nope. Can't get more 'til Thursday. Bet you've got some allotment to spare, though."

I tugged back, but for a tiny man who spent most of his allocation on booze, he had remarkable strength. My fingers itched for the gun, but with my right arm trapped in Matthias' grip, I couldn't reach it. The pistol taunted me, pressing into my hip where he'd pulled me against the stall.

Bracing my feet, I leaned back and yanked hard, pulling his upper body onto the counter. He didn't let go. People behind him in the line surged forward shouting their anger. "Thief. Thief."

Three red-uniformed guards rushed in from different parts of the market, grabbed the would-be thief, and dragged him into the center of the small clearing.

They beat Matthias long after he quit fighting back. Horror coiled in my stomach and threatened to spew my morning meal over the last three apples. As they dragged Matthias' limp form away, I looked up and found George waiting at the front of the line.

"Seems the lovely guards, there, managed to divert a few of your patrons in their peace-keeping duties." He slid back an oversized sleeve and held out his wrist. The scanner beeped. I handed him one apple and slipped a second one into the sleeve of his coat.

Granny Foster got the last one.

The hollow gaze of the next person in line, the one pegged by the people as the fastest slowpoke, used to haunt me. The passage of time and the inability to change the altered order of our existence taught me to avert my gaze. Just slam the shutters and huddle in the warmth of the shack's heater until the crowd dispersed.

As I locked up, a rap on the rear door sent my heart skittering. I patted the gun and slid open the peep hole. The Market Regulation Commander, Raymond Grubbs, stood outside, his bald head gleaming in the light of the mid-morning sun.

"Grace, your numbers are off. Open up." His voice sounded gruff and deep, a sound that used to make us chuckle.

Before the Even Stephen Laws, Raymond's high squeaky voice rang out over the ice skating rink's loudspeaker announcing special treats at the concession stand or time for couples' skating. Like many of the fringes of society, people the new laws aimed to help, he ended up with a high-level position. It didn't take him long to force his voice deeper when he spoke as an official. Rumor had it, he spent most evenings drinking stolen lemon and honey to ease the daily cases of laryngitis.

I eased the door open, faking a look of innocence and frustration over the loss of an apple sale.

He stomped into the shack and glanced around. The space, small as it was, seemed to shrink with his sizable bulk crammed inside. Everyone knew he skimmed off the top, but all the commanders did it. Each one fatter than the next.

"You should have sold one hundred, but the allotments total ninety-nine. Surely your father's orchard still bears fruit?"

We had fruit. Bushels of it. Most of it rotting. No matter how much we lowered the portion cost, our trees produced too much. My uncle hid the extra in fear of the authorities discovering it and declaring our farm and trees community property, one more livelihood destroyed by the infamous greedy Stephen who started this mess.

"You heard about Matthias?" My voice quivered with nerves as I asked. Maybe he'd attribute it to anxiety over the attack.

"Yes, yes. Sorry thing. You won't have to worry about him, though. Shipping him off to the stocks. He'll get plenty of apples there. If he can catch them with his teeth." A wheeze of laughter shook the man for a moment before he exploded in a coughing fit.

I shrank from the flying spittle and drew my scarf around my nose and mouth. I couldn't afford to be sick, dependent on old wives' tales to heal me. No one wanted to be doctors anymore. What was the use? The doctors who could afford the officials' bribes found jobs in Canada before the government closed the borders. They fled this crazed society in droves.

Grubbs' coughing fit finally died out. "Harrumph. Apologies Grace." He studied a black rectangle on a band around his wrist, the Portion Monitor.

It reminded me of the Smart Watch I'd gotten for my sixteenth birthday just weeks before Congress passed Even Stephen. I still have it, not that it works. Not much does work, anymore. No one wants to put in a grueling day's labor when they give us our allotment each week, anyway. Why bother?

"Now the question of your missing portion?" His gray eyes studied notes on his monitor.

I sighed with relief. If he suspected something, he'd look me in the eye, crowd his flabby body up against me in the shack.

"I'm afraid it got smashed underfoot when the guards came to take Matthias."

"Hm?" He lifted his face to look at me. "Oh, yes. I see. Then I guess the guards owe you a portion." He tapped something on the monitor, his brow wrinkled, then he nodded. "Balance looks good. See you on Friday."

I closed the door behind him and slumped against the wall.

When I stepped outside later, only a few stall owners remained, closing up shop. The leaves whipped by my feet and twirled above the ground on a cool gust of wind. I paused to breathe in the crisp autumn air. Isabella, the chicken farmer's daughter, wandered over, a smile on her lips. "You had some excitement today, Grace."

I shrugged, the joy of the season's simplicity lost to an awareness of why she sought me out.

"Mind if I walk with you?" She fell in step with me without waiting for a response.

We started down the path, our feet not falling in synch as most people's do when they stroll together. I waited for what I knew was coming. She wanted details.

"So did Matthias really yank you out of the stall?"

The quick shift from truth to rumor shocked my feet to a standstill like a doe I spied in the meadow the other day, caught unaware and unsure which way to run. "What? No. Nothing like that."

Somehow, I must find a way to divert her attention. My family stood together in our resolve to not share in the village's ugly gossip.

"Did you sell out of eggs early?" I said, as I started walking up the uneven road again, stepping over weed-filled cracks.

She nodded. "Our prime layer is turning out nothing good. I wandered around after that." She peered at me, a shy smile on her face. "With Billy."

Billy, one of the Regulators who beat Matthias, used to be a quarterback in college. That's why he became a Regulator. They recruited athletes, former military, and weightlifters, the physically strong. My brother turned them down. That's when Isabella broke off her engagement to him. She wanted someone worthy of the new government. I wasn't surprised she'd picked Billy. He came back from training all puffed up with importance, and many of the girls took notice.

As we ambled past the crumbling mansions of the once wealthy, Isabella said, "Got any spoilage from your trees? A bunch of us are going down to the stocks later. Pop has some rotten eggs. Thought we'd have a little fun. You could get some revenge. I'm sure Matthias would appreciate the offering." She snorted, the sound echoing Raymond's sleazy laugh. It interrupted the quiet morning air, sending a murder of crows in flight from the towering oaks sheltering our route.

Isabella used to be sweet. Then again, so did most of us.

When they passed the law, my philosophy teacher, George, speculated society would go this route. Just a few weeks after Congress made it official, I witnessed my first stockade prisoner getting pummeled by spoiled food and clods of mud. Neighbors I'd once respected, now ugly and vengeful, screamed and shouted their fury at his crime. All he'd done was express concern over how the Even Stephen law determined our wages, the equal amount each person received to live on.

Fighting back tears of horror, I had rushed away from the mob in the square that day and stumbled over George as he ran toward the scene, a frown of determination tarnishing his kind features. At the sight of my tears, he had stopped. "Grace? Are you hurt?"

I wiped at my face and shook my head. Voices screeched from the square reminding me of a frenzied group of chimpanzees I'd seen in the zoo once. George winced and turned toward the square. I could see he wanted to go, but he hesitated to leave me.

"Are you ok? Do you need me to walk you home?" He looked behind him again as the sound grew shriller. "If not, I must go. Someone should try to stop this foolishness."

I wondered what a man his age could do, but that was a few years before they beat the fire of rebellion out of him. "I'm fine. Go."

But as he started to turn away, I couldn't hold back my thoughts. "How did you know? It's just as you said."

Determination faded from his face, and his shoulders sagged under the weight of sadness that clouded his eyes. "Everything comes back around," he'd said. "History proves that time and again. Just another nasty consequence Congress failed to consider."

Isabella's bright voice drew me back to the road and our walk from the square. "Well? Do you want to go? I've been practicing my throwing arm for weeks. I'm pretty good. In fact, I've got a bet with Billy that I can land an egg between Matthias' eyes."

I looked at Isabella's cheerful smile, excitement burning in her gaze at the idea of torturing Matthias.

"No thanks," I said with a shudder. Playing to the shudder, I added, "I think I'm catching a cold."

My brother, Sean, taught me this trick to avoid unwanted attention or questionable entertainment. No one dared come in contact with a sick person. The herbal woman's cures sometimes worked but often didn't. Even when they did, the concoctions were nasty.

Isabella sidestepped and wrapped her scarf around her face. "Oh well. You best get on home. I think I forgot something back at Daddy's stall."

Her feet carried her away at a frantic clip.

I smiled to myself. Sometimes fear worked the other way around. Kept the heathens at bay.

I trudged on toward home, thankful to survive another day mostly unscathed.

Authors Note: I wrote "Even Stephen Heathens" in response to a contest prompt to write a story where all people receive the same income. It didn't win because I didn't portray a Utopian world. The winner did. I feel like this is more realistic. Do you?

4

Not-A-Nut

Sometimes a nut isn't all it's cracked up to be. I ponder this as I gaze down from my beautiful oak tree. This man, the one pacing around and around my home, seems to be looking for the perfect one. Strange man. He never looks up, only at the ground.

I chitter and swish my glorious long tail. Good luck dude.

He won't find any decent nuts unless he climbs my tree, way above this branch perch, to get a shot at my stash. Not that I'd let him. Nu-uh. I did the work. They're all mine, squirreled away in my hiding place.

Now cracked shells? Yup. There's plenty of them down there. He can have all the fragments he wants.

Just the idea makes me crave a snack. With one last glance, I hop to higher branches, grab a lovely morsel, and make quick work of its shell.

The man jumps as my discarded fragments pelt him. Ha ha. Yes. I have them. Go find your own tree. My tail ripples with joy as I shove the whole nut in my mouth.

I've never understood why humans want our food anyway. The brown shells they bring to the park contain enough for them. The crinkly noises they make cracking open those shells only brag to us about their gathering skills. A lot of interesting fragrances float up to me when they pop them open, too. The long, skinny sticks covered in tiny white specks are my favorites. I heard one woman call them "fries." I don't care what they're called, they're goo—ood. Why take our food? I chitter my confusion.

Then, there's the really big stashes like this man carried with him. It's huge and looks like tree branches woven together. They usually appear in the flowering season, though, not during gathering time. All sorts of food come out of them and some weird ground thing they sit on. I scampered across one once while the humans ran around throwing a flat thing at each other. Soft, really soft, but my claws got stuck. I thought I'd never escape.

The man pauses, then bends over staring at something. He drops to the ground, his skinny claws sliding through the leaves. "No, no, no." They make that sound a lot.

He looks funny crouched like a squirrel but with no tail for balance. And yep, he's tilted too far and now plops to the ground, his paws running through the fur on top of his head. Don't get me started on the lack of fur. What's up with that, anyway?

His whispers get louder, moaning like the wind does through my home's branches. Most humans laugh or chitter or remain silent. I don't think I've ever seen the male species do this.

I hop to a lower branch to investigate. He doesn't notice, so I drop to the ground but shy away from the sneaky edge of his ground cover.

"I can't believe I lost it." He turns his arm in that weird way humans do to stare at a shimmering thing on his wrist, then he rubs his paws through his fur again. "She'll be here soon. What a disaster."

I inch closer. A lost nut? Gotta be. What else could create such distress? I'd like to find a nut that special. Shove it to the back of my tree stash to save until the white stuff lies thick on the ground.

Since I'm closer, I sniff toward his stash. No fries.

The man looks up but doesn't jump away. Weird. Most of them do or try to catch me. "Have you seen it, pretty one?"

I creep closer.

"Of course not." His claws rake through his fur again. "It's shiny. Not a nut. But about the right size."

Something shiny? Raven takes the shinies. Searching the branches, I think I spot her. Did she take his not-a-nut? Doesn't sound tasty, but Raven likes weird human things, not just food.

The breeze blows and leaves scrape and scratch the ground. I jump back to my tree, climb the trunk, and perch on a low branch.

The man ignores my exit, paws sweeping through the leaves again.

A gust of wind flutters his soft ground cover. Something flashes.

Claws gripping the bark, I race down the trunk toward the glitter. I search. Where? The sun glints through the branches, and I see the flash again, right next to the man's big paw. Skitter to it and scoop it up. Taste it. Yuck.

The whistle of wind through wings gives me brief warning, and I bounce toward the man just before Raven lands where I was. She cocks her head at me. "Squawk."

The man stumbles backward, staring at Raven. I leap to his shoulder before she can see what I hold. His body tenses, gaze darting between me and Raven. Then his eyes grow large as he stares at his not-a-nut in my teeth.

"Justin?" A high-pitched voice calls out.

This human freezes, like the statues near the water, but not cold like them.

Raven complains at the interruption and, with a big flap, soars into the branches.

I cling to the man's shoulder as he spins to meet her. She holds one of those big white shells in one paw. The delicious scent of fries floats toward me. I like her.

"Um." She bites her lip. "You have a squirrel on your shoulder."

"Do I?" His voice sounds better, not whispery or frantic.

The woman takes a step closer, and I launch myself toward the enticing fries smell, the not-a-nut still held between my teeth. Her shoulder covering is softer than his. I sniff toward the bag. Fries and flowers. I don't see flowers, though.

She doesn't scream or smack me. I like her.

"Hi little guy. What do you have there?" She looks at the not-a-nut. "Justin?

The man tumbles to his knees in front of her. "Marry me?"

She laughs. "You trained a squirrel?"

He leans closer. "Will he give it to you?"

We study each other, she with her large, sky-colored eyes and me with my perfect squirrel gaze. I've never given something to a human, but she wants the not-a-nut. I can tell.

The white nut in her paw crinkles, and the man pulls "fries" from it. "Trade?"

I drop the not-a-nut, grab the fries, and jump to a branch. Salty goodness fills my mouth while the man takes the not-a-nut and puts it on one of her claws.

Weird, but that's humans for you.

Author's Note: I needed a short story for my February 2024 newsletter. I wrote this one quickly and have updated it a good bit since that newsletter came out. It's light on tension, but I love its simplicity.

5

Whippoorwill Calling

"Yahh! That's cold!" Dana fell back on the dock as she yanked her feet out of the lake, splashing us in the process.

We laughed. The cool water came as a welcome change after a long, hot summer. The four of us—Dana, Mary, Mary's mother, and myself—sat on a dock beside Lake Jocassee listening to the sounds of evening float across the water. A breeze drifted over the lake and chilled my bare arms. As I stared at my reflection in the murky depths, a lone whippoorwill sang out. "Whippoorwill ... Whippoorwill." The last note lingered on the still air.

I shivered. "I heard that whippoorwill last night."

Mary's mother—we called her by her first name, Rose—nodded. "Some people say they foretell death."

I shivered again.

Dana flicked at the water with her toes, sending splatters across the surface. "I thought that was owls," she said.

"Them too." A smile flitted across Rose's broad face.

The whippoorwill called again, "Whippoorwill...Whippoorwill."

"Whippoorwills sound plain spooky to me," I whispered, ashamed that my voice quivered.

To my surprise, they agreed.

"The whole house is creepy," Dana said. "It feels haunted."

Rose had rented the lake cottage for an end of summer fling before her daugher's last year of high school. The old house sat on a small peninsula that rose above the lake. The rooms were dark, furnished with heavy, antique furniture, and decorated with a taxidermist's eye to decor. It creeped me out. Even the antiques unnerved me, reminders of ghosts lurking nearby, protecting their treasured objects.

"It's like something's watching us in there," I said.

Mary muttered something and then jumped to her feet. "Ya'll are no fun." She stalked up the hill. After a moment, Rose clambered up the hill after her daughter, calling out to her to wait.

I watched Mary walk away, feeling superior in my willingness to stay. A wicked thought crossed my mind. I turned to Dana. "Ya know Mary's afraid of wardrobe closets. She thinks something'll jump out at her. There's one in our room."

It was the first thing I noticed when we chose bedrooms the night before. Dana snored, so she got a room to herself. That left Mary and me in the room with the wardrobe closet.

Until Mary told me about her fear, I never gave wardrobes another thought. Mary's power of suggestion, though, was all I needed to set off my crazy imagination. I don't know which scared me more: the whippoorwill calling, the animal corpses decorating every corner of the house, the antiques, or that looming wardrobe closet.

Dana laughed out loud. "Wouldn't it be funny if..." She paused and watched me, her eyes dancing.

We stared at each other for a moment, and then I laughed.

While Mary and Rose wandered the shoreline, we hatched our plan. It sounded simple: wait until bedtime, distract Mary, and then slip Dana into the closet.

Just because something sounds easy doesn't mean it is. Once Dana was in the closet, she couldn't move without making a lot of noise.

Suppressing our giggles and whispers, we dragged an old metal step stool into the bedroom and wedged it tightly into the small space in the closet. It left just enough room for Dana to tuck herself inside. We tested it. No noise.

"Are you ready?" I whispered to her.

She smiled and gave me a thumbs up. I closed the door, watching her face disappear as I shut out the light. My chest constricted at the solid click, like I had just closed her into a sarcophagus.

Averting my eyes from the frozen animal corpses that lined the hall, I hurried to the bathroom. I peed with my eyes shut, avoiding the steady gaze of the huge, stuffed owl perched on a shelf across from the toilet.

* * *

Lights out. The dark enveloped us, and I lay waiting. Clouds rode across the face of the moon casting shadows on the walls. Tree branches danced in the night, scratching against the roof. Water slapped against the floating dock, a hollow plunking sound. The house became its dark, creepy self again, and my stomach churned in anticipation.

Several minutes passed and Mary's breathing developed the regular rhythm of sleep. The whippoorwill's song sought out souls in the night. "Whippoorwill ...Whippoorwill."

All I could think was, *Get it over with*, but Dana was silent. I tried to imagine how she felt entombed in the darkness, and I was glad to be in the bed instead. Every time I closed my eyes, I saw her face disappear behind the lid of a coffin followed by the accusing eyes of the stuffed owl in the bathroom.

The longer I lay there, the more I questioned our plan. I was ready to confess when I heard a scratching from the closet.

Then Dana moaned, low and long.

Mary sat up. "What was that?"

"I don't know." A pulse of adrenaline raced through me. *What was Dana doing? I thought the plan was to just jump out.*

Dana moaned again. "Aaaahhhh, Oooohhhhh."

Mary whimpered and pulled the covers to her chin.

Thump, Thump, THUMP, came from the closet.

A thrill of fear rolled over me. *Why didn't Dana get it over with?*

"Aaaaahhhhhh!" Scratch, thump, thump. "Unhhhhh!" THUMP. THUMP. BANG!

The closet rocked. The door rattled, and then something fell against the door and shrieked down it, like nails on a chalkboard.

My hair stood on end. Mary cried and buried her head under the sheets.

Everything went quiet. Seconds ticked by.

"Whippoorwill ... Whippoorwill." The bird's death call floated through the air.

In the distance, another answered. "Whippoorwill ... Whip-poorwill."

Silence, like its own voice, rang through the room. The wind blew. The old house creaked and groaned.

Mary sobbed.

This was too much. I opened my mouth to tell Dana to come out, but no sound came forth. My throat closed up just like in my worst nightmares. I clawed at the covers, ready to jump up and open the closet. The sheets tangled around my legs, entrapping me. I kicked at them, unable to get free.

The closet erupted with furious thumps and bangs. "Let me ou-utttt!"

"Let ME outttttt!"

"LET ME OUT!" The door burst open and Dana flung herself on top of Mary. "I've got you!"

Mary screamed.

I felt the bed sway. A loud crack sounded below me. The bed frame crashed to the floor. BANG!

I tried to scream, but my voice still hid in my throat.

Dana's triumphant laughter and Mary's screams echoed through the house until light flooded the room.

Rose stood in the doorway shaking her head at the destruction.

The bed sat at a twisted angle, leaning toward the wardrobe closet.

Mary cried and flailed at Dana.

Rose captured her daughter's arms and grabbed her in a bear hug. "Shh. It's OK, it's OK."

Mary peered over her mother's shoulder at us. Her eyes hardened as she caught sight of Dana. "You!" She fought to free herself from her mother's arms, but Rose held her tight.

Dana laughed harder.

Mary stopped her struggles, but her eyes stared at us in pain. "It's not funny, it's not funny."

* * *

The next morning, I rose early. Picking at a splinter under my fingernail, I shuffled into the kitchen. Dana stared out the window.

I punched her arm. "What was all that last night?"

Dana rubbed her arm and scowled at me. "What was what?"

"All that thumping and scratching," I said. "Ohhhh. Ahhhh. Let me out. Let me out!" I mimicked in a high-pitched voice.

Dana stared at me. "What are you talking about?"

"You! In the closet! Making all that noise. You took long enough." I slammed a coffee cup on the counter.

Dana shook her head, confusion wrinkling her forehead."Beth, I didn't say anything. I couldn't make any noises. The door stuck. I thought I'd never get out of there."

"Come on," I said, still plucking at the splinter under my fingernail. "You expect me to believe that you didn't make any noises in that closet?"

"Yes." Dana's gaze held the conviction of truth. I knew her well enough to believe her.

"Then w hat?" F ear t raced c old d own m y b ack. I y anked the splinter free. Blood pooled on my fingertip.

I ran to the closet and yanked open the door. Two sets of long, fresh gouges ran down the length of the wood. My fingertips fit them perfectly.

Author's Note: I'm sorry if you never see wardrobe closets or hear the call of a whippoorwill again without trepidation.
This story first appeared in *The Petigru Review*.

6

A Good Trade

The green and yellow sinuous lines rippled along the curves of the paperclip and drew me like a magnet. My hand hovered. The lines coiled and undulated, and I snatched my hand back, fingers curled against my heart. In the background, the copy machine whirred, shuffling and collating my document.

It was nothing but a simple paper clip.

But not really so simple. Paperclips like this one, decorated with elaborate swirls that mimicked motion, cost extra, definitely not standard office-issue.

I cast a furtive glance toward the corridor. The hall stood empty. No one rounded the corner in a breathless rush searching for this special office supply.

The copy machine sighed its final breath as the last page slid onto the pile of collated and stapled documents. I bit my lip and turned away from the temptation lying on the table. Before I could change my mind, I gathered up originals and duplicates and hurried down the hallway.

It was just a paperclip, right? So why did I want to turn back and get it? Why did it pull at me, taunting me like a hot brownie sundae?

* * *

Two days later, I returned to the scene of temptation and found it waiting for me. Same spot. Same position. I grabbed it, clenched in my fist, and rushed back to my office. At my desk, I studied the clean green and yellow lines on the paperclip. I caressed it. Satisfaction rolled through me. If someone truly wanted to keep this paperclip, they wouldn't have left it there. Not for two days.

With a shake of my head, I tried to clear my greedy thoughts and placed the clip at the top of my desk blotter. The glow from my lamp embraced it, making the lines of color ripple and gyrate.

"I'm going crazy," I told myself, dropping my face into my hands.

"Well," a deep voice said, "talking to yourself is a sure sign of insanity."

I jerked upright and spun my chair toward the door.

Brad pushed his equipment cart into the room and leaned against the door frame. A hot blush crept up my neck as I appraised his overall effect—thick dark hair sweeping across a strong forehead, piercing blue eyes the color of the Caribbean Sea, a firm jaw line and broad shoulders. A more perfect male specimen did not exist.

I shrugged. "I guess I'm certifiable. You won't tell anyone, will you?"

"It'll cost you, Evie." Brad cocked his head to the side and winked.

I'd feel flattered if he didn't flirt with all the women in the office the same way.

I crossed my arms over my chest in mock severity. "That depends. What did you have in mind?"

From his cart, he pulled out a large, lumpy, paper sack. "My mom went apple picking and sent me bushels. I'm trying to unload them."

He extended the bag toward me, face transforming into an imitation of a begging Oliver, about to say, "Please sir, can I have some more?"

No man should know he's that adorable.

"What kind?" I stalled, knowing anything Brad offered I'd take.

Muscles flexed under his white dress shirt as he pulled a perfect specimen from the bag and extended it like the witch in Snow White. "Gala. Like a party in your mouth."

I bit back the evil retort and accepted the bag of apples. "Remember, I'm buying your silence."

"Of course." He saluted and pushed his cart down the hall. I leaned forward and enjoyed his exit.

Humming a happy tune, I turned back to my desk and dropped the bag on the surface. One perfectly shaped apple spilled out and rolled over to the paperclip. It halted, resting against the curved wire, and called to me with a siren's appeal. My mouth watered, and I licked my lips.

Somehow, I'd missed lunch. Again.

One crunch and sweet apple goodness filled my senses. Juice dripped down my chin, and the crisp flesh squeaked against my teeth with each bite. Leaning back in the desk chair, I swiveled and snacked—until my gaze fell on my stolen object. Before I knew it, the paperclip lay clutched in my hand again.

"Why do you plague me?" I said.

The ridges of its colored lines dimpled my palm as I squeezed it. The tip dug into my skin. I took another bite. Blood welled along my lifeline.

Thunder cracked and lightning flashed. I spun toward the window. Clear blue sky greeted me. I lurched from the chair and searched the street below. Vertigo struck and my stomach contracted, dropping me to my knees with a gasp. Curled in a ball on the cold floor, I moaned in agony. Deep breaths did little to ease the pain. The room tilted; bile rose in my throat. Eyes closed, I groped for my chair.

Then...

The spasm ceased without warning. I dragged my head up, drawing in deep breaths. Fresh, earthy aromas filled my nose. My hand grasped rough edges. Tree bark?

Sunlight filtered between the greenest leaves. The air smelled clean. Sweet. Intoxicating. Sun spilled glorious warmth over my skin while birds sang with joy.

I lifted my face to the sky and inhaled. A cacophony of floral scents flooded my nostrils. Flowers tipped in the light breeze, the colors clearer and brighter than any I'd ever seen.

"Beautiful," I said, my voice light and carefree.

The paperclip's ridges slid along my bare legs.

Bare legs?

I jerked as if waking. A green- and yellow-striped creature nestled on my lower leg, its skin rippling. Stubby limbs stuck out at odd angles from its body. Scales coiled, bunched, and re-stretched, inching the creature up my inner-calf muscle. At my sudden gasp, the four-legged thing turned a pointed snout toward me.

"Greetingssss."

The soft grass gave me pause when I scooted back, shaking my leg.

"You!" I pointed at the creature in accusation. A perfect, un-eaten apple flew from my fingertips.

"Yesss?"

"It's a dream," I said, hiding my chest under handfuls of my hair, more thick and luxurious than it should be.

The creature half-crawled, half-undulated toward me. "Not a dream, Evie. Welcome to the Garden." It cocked its head sideways, glancing through the bushes. "Ahh, your help meet approaches. I'll leave you to get to know him." It winked, then slid-crawled in the other direction, disappearing among the flowers.

"Eve! Why do you sit here?" A man approached.

I gasped. Whip-fast, I drew my legs to my chest and wrapped my arms around my knees.

He plopped down next to me, casual and comfortable. His hand reached up and traced a line down my arm. Goose flesh followed the track.

If this was a dream, it sure felt real. I peered sideways, studying his face, studiously refusing to look lower.

"Brad?" I leaned forward in surprise.

"What's brad?" He tilted his head to the right. "Have you named another flower?"

I scooted backward, all the while staring at his sweep of dark hair and startling Caribbean-blue eyes. Just like the flowers, this man radiated more beauty than Brad could ever possess, yet my co-worker's essence lingered in his smile.

Such a simple smile. It twinkled in his eyes and drew me in.

The man hopped to his feet. "Come on." He extended a hand. "You know He waits to walk with us."

I tightened my arms around my knees, fighting the urge to take his hand and follow him anywhere. "Who?"

"Have you been talking to the owls again, Eve? You act so strange." The smile fell from his face, and he dragged me to my feet. Such strength. "You know we don't speak owl to each other, only to them."

A gentle hand caressed my cheek, and I fought the urge to lean into him.

He glanced toward the tree's branches above us, a flash of concern storming in his eyes. "Or is it this tree? Why do you choose to sit under this tree?"

I glanced upward, unsure of why that particular tree might be a problem. It hung heavy with round, red fruit. I knew I should recognize them, but as I stared upward time spiraled through the leaves. I swayed, unsteady on my feet. Strong arms caught me. I faltered and grabbed his arm. Sparks shot up my fingers, and I fought to recall why I shouldn't be there; why our skin touching dismayed me. I grasped at something far and distant in my thoughts. A strange memory of metal and technology...

"Adam, what is metal?" The word felt harsh and wrong. "Or tek nawl a gee?"

A bark of laughter escaped his lips and he glanced around at the luscious plant-life surrounding us. "Eve. You've been naming plants again, haven't you? I thought we were going to do that together."

The smile he flashed at me exhibited more love than I could absorb.

"We must hurry." He took my hand. "I hear Him calling to us. You can show me what you named later."

In the distance, I heard a voice like none other calling. "Adam! Eve!"

* * *

The strange, coiling, four-legged creature found me every time I left Adam's side.

"Greetingssss, Adam's help meet."

"Why do you call me that?" I leaned forward and extended a tentative finger along its slithery, green and yellow skin.

It lifted slitted eyes toward me, a forked tongue flashing in and out of the slash of a mouth at the end of its snout. *"That's what you are. Have Adam and He not told you?"*

I searched my memory, but little stuck there beside the lush garden we called home. Soothing days flooded into restful nights and love surrounded me. Peace drenched my senses. Somewhere in the recesses of my mind, I knew I had not always felt this way. But the feeling evaporated every time Adam or He spoke to me.

"Ahh" The creature's head bobbed in a strange swaying way. "They keep so much from you."

"I have everything. Why would you claim such a thing?" A bird called from the branches of a tree and I wandered toward it, aware that the green and yellow creature followed behind me.

The head swiveled and swayed. *"Everything?"*

"Of course. Look." The bird fluttered down and perched on my finger. She chirped and sang a joyous song, then flew away.

I turned toward the creature. "There is nothing I can't enjoy."

With a wink, the creature turned and undulated into the heart of the garden. "Follow me."

The tree loomed above all others, beautiful green leaves waving in the breeze, large red fruit dangling from the branches.

"What of this tree?" the creature asked.

"I can sit beneath its branches and rest. Its fragrance fills my nose with sweet aroma."

For a face unable to show expressions, the creature managed to regard me with disgust. "And what of the fruit?"

My heart thumped in alarm. "No." I shook my head and backed away.

"Why?" It slithered after me.

"It's the tree of death. He said not to eat of it. No good will come of it."

"*No.*" The creature scrabbled its short front limbs up my calf, scratching the flesh with sharp claws.

"Ouch!" I shook my leg, but it clung to me.

"You will not die. This is why I brought you here; your love and desire for what tantalizes you. Your lust for forbidden fruit."

The words confused me. Forbidden? Desire? Tantalize? I didn't know these words.

"She wouldn't do it, so I found you." It inched one claw further up my leg.

"She? I am she." Claws dug deeper into my leg, and I struggled to shake the creature free. I collapsed to the ground in a heap. "Let go of me."

"*Very well.*" It dropped to the ground and settled in the grass before me. "You speak correctly. You are she." Its tongue darted out to clean red fluid from a claw.

The welts on my leg leaked the same red. I dabbed at the liquid, a rush of fear filling my center. "What is this?"

"Your lifesource. It flows throughout your body. Without it, you die."

Its tongue flicked out and licked more red from a clawed foot.

"Give it back!" I grabbed at the creature, but it slid out of reach.

Its mouth stretched wide in a caricature of a smile. "Your body must make more. The red fruit will help. But you must eat of it."

Lifesource trickled down my leg, draining from my body. It throbbed where the creature's claws had punctured my skin. A handful of leaves didn't staunch the flow. I rushed to the stream and washed, horrified as the clear water clouded red. More life-source flowed from me.

The creature called to me from a low branch on the tree. *"Here is a good one. Just one bite will cure you. You will not die."*

I ran to the tree.

The fruit came free from the branch with ease, its smooth red flesh waiting to give me back my lifesource.

I bit.

* * *

The floor of my office felt gritty and cold against my cheek. My head pounded and a shrill sound rang in my ears. I sat up, the apple still clutched in my hand. A weight pressed down on me, and I cried out in pain at the loss of pure ecstasy. Limp hair hung over my face and I shoved it behind my ears in disgust.

Each drag of air suffocated my soul, each breath a struggle to inhale. I clambered upright, using the desk as support. The room's light shone gray and dim, lackluster. Institutional smells assaulted me.

"A dream," I told myself.

My leg stung, and I shrieked in horror at the snake wrapped around my calf, teeth embedded in my skin. It slithered down my leg, leaving a chill in its path, and dropped to the floor. The creature raised its head above the ground. "My legsss for your soul. A good trade."

It coiled in on itself and disappeared.

I brushed my hand over my eyes and slumped against the desk. Gashes on my leg leaked blood, my lifesource. It puddled in a red pool on the floor.

Beside a plain, everyday-issue, paperclip.

Author's Note: The inspiration for "A Good Trade" was an actual paperclip with green and yellow lines. At the time I wrote this, patterns on paperclips were new and expensive, so I was intrigued when I saw one abandoned in the copy room where I worked. When it was still there a week later, I took it. I still have it. Amazing where story inspirations spring from! Although not my first published short story, it is the first *fantasy* short story I got published. It appeared under the title "Lifesource" in the online anthology, *Stupefying Stories*.

7

Buggers

Enid needed coffee. Odd for someone who only drank water, but everyone had an off day here and then.

The clock on the far wall of the production floor read 9:58. Two minutes to break. She groaned and picked up a gasket from the conveyor and almost fumbled it. The air she breathed stuck in her throat. Suffocating. Wrong. Like a cloud pressing down on her. It had started the moment she'd arrived for her shift at Henley's.

She inspected another gasket. Glanced at the clock: 9:59.

Ignoring the conveyor, she willed the second hand forward.

When the break buzzer rang, she jumped off her stool, turning to find Ramone, her replacement, waiting to take over.

"No scrap, no rework, so far," she told him, forcing a lightness in her tone.

He switched places with her and nodded, eyes already trained on the conveyor, and repeated the plant's mantra. "With Mighty Enid at the helm, nothing would dare go wrong."

She gave a half-hearted smile and turned away. Tastebuds salivating for a large, hot cup of black coffee.

Before she could take two steps, her phone buzzed. She unclipped it and checked the screen before answering. "Enid."

"Hey Enid." The syrupy voice of June in Human Resources sent prickles of warning down her back. Whenever June turned up the flavor in her voice, it meant she needed something.

"Hi June." An unexpected urge to scowl hit Enid and tinged her voice. *What in the world is wrong with me?*

After a pause, June blurted her message. "Will needs you to come to his office. New employee."

"Now?" Goodbye coffee.

"Yes."

"Sure. Be there in two." She jammed the phone back into her belt clip.

Sometimes being Mighty Enid sucked. Most times, it didn't. Being the hero came easy when you didn't have to do anything but show up for work and make people laugh and smile. No one knew her secret. Grandpa made sure of that.

"Never tell anyone," he'd warned many years ago, his dark brown eyes piercing deep into her six-year-old soul like he could see through to her toes. "They won't believe you. Only you can see those nasty buggers. They'll come after you if they get a sniff of what you can do. You don't want that."

At the time, Grandpa's warning scared the be-jeezus out of her, but over the years, she'd realized the wisdom in his words. He'd raised her after her mother died. When she was twelve, he told her the buggers killed her dad before she was born. He'd tried to stop them from overwhelming passengers on a Greyhound bus. Real heroes paid the price.

She accepted his warning. And now she found it easier to live under the fake reputation of heroism than try to be the real thing.

Her mantra, *run away*, worked. Every time she saw any of the tiny yellow buggers, no matter what damage they wrought, she did a quick about-face in retreat.

"Hey Enid." John, a line supervisor, fell in step with her. "They call you upstairs?"

"Sure did." Enid forced more energy into her voice and prayed John didn't catch a hint of anything but satisfaction.

"Guess you're going to train the new employee. Can't have her upsetting paradise."

"Nope." Unable to fake her normal chitchat, Enid picked up her pace. "Gotta run."

Yes, paradise. This plant was hers. Until she discovered this little town of homegrown locals and its main employer, Henley's Gaskets, she'd struggled to find a safe place. To stay off the buggers' radar. With not a bugger in sight, no hint of their mischief, she'd found a home.

Henley's did well, but once she became team lead, their quality skyrocketed. Everyone refused to listen when she claimed no responsibility. Small towns lived on gossip. And legend.

If they only knew.

The cool whoosh of air conditioning flooded over her as she left production and pushed through the heavy, vacuum-sealed doors. She headed for HR, her steel-toed boots hushed by the navy-blue carpet runner. Unlike the clinical white of production, the office area sported sunshine-yellow walls, gray slate floor tiles under the carpet runner, and piped-in instrumental music. It might be nice if it wasn't for the walls. The yellow unnerved her, too much like her nemesis. Today, it clawed at her skin.

Hopefully, Will could fill her in quickly. Then she'd chug a swallow or two of caffeine to set her right.

June, the forty-something bleached-blond daughter of the mayor, looked up from her computer as Enid walked in. She mouthed *"I'm sorry"* before greeting her out loud. "Hey Enid. Will said to sit tight. He got an emergency call right after I talked to you."

Will's door was shut. Unusual.

"Emergency?" Concern skittered up Enid's back. Will had a newborn just out of the NICU. "Is everything ok with the baby?"

June shook her head. "Baby's fine. The emergency's not at home." She leaned forward, eyes wide. "It's here."

The skittering galloped straight to Enid's heart. Nothing went wrong at Henley's. Not since she'd been here. That's why everyone called her Mighty Enid. Five years of no accidents, no arguments, no drops in sales or production. Just the opposite.

Before Enid could draw another breath, June's phone rang. She turned to answer, pausing as several of the buttons on the switchboard sparked to life. "Oh my." June punched the first one. "HR, can you hold, please?" She froze, then gasped, and did not press HOLD. "Where? How many?"

She wrote something on a notepad, the scratch of the pen on paper rasping and loud. Ignoring the blinking lights, she stared up at Enid, face growing pale, her eyes wide with shock.

Enid rushed to the desk. "June? What is it?"

The notepad June held up had four large letters slashed across the page: R A T S.

It couldn't be. Had the buggers found her? Lured vermin to aid in their destruction? Enid looked around the office for signs of her yellow enemies lurking in the corners. Nothing.

Will's office door flew open. When his gaze fell on Enid, he sagged against the doorjamb like a forlorn balloon days after a party. "I forgot about you."

"What's going on?" She took in his disheveled appearance—tie askew, hair sticking up like sprouts of asparagus, one shirt sleeve rolled up, the other unbuttoned and dangling.

The lights flashing on June's phone snatched Will's attention. "June?"

The poor woman's hand trembled as she pointed to the note she'd shown Enid.

Will took one long look at the four letters. "What does this mean?"

"They've got rats in the clean room."

He ran a hand through his hair. Nodded toward the blinking lights. "What's with those calls?"

"I've never had more than one call on hold. I'm not sure how to handle this many." She bit her lip. "Even if I could, I'm not sure I want to."

Looking between June and Will, Enid's stomach bunched into a knot—the kind that took several patient hours to unpick. The two appeared shellshocked. Nothing desperate ever happened at Henley's, so what was going on? She checked the corners of the office again. With yellow walls, the buggers might blend in. Still, she found nothing.

Will crowded behind June's chair, took the headset, and punched a button. "Is this an emergency?" He paused. "We know."

He punched the next button and repeated the same conversation. On the fifth call, his follow up changed. "Marnie? Great. Did you catch the snake?"

Fearing the answer, Enid turned to June. "Where is the new employee?"

June sighed, her eyes reflecting regret. "Trilly? Such a sweet girl. I hate this happened on her first day. I'd quit if I were her. With all that's happened. Will sent her to machine prep. When the snake showed up, he sent her to Hector."

Hector. The clean room where they now had rats. Cold assuredness squeezed the breath from Enid's lungs.

"Don't hire her." Enid turned to Will who stood staring at the phone.

He looked up, blinking a counter-rhythm to the still-flashing lines. "Already have. Done deal."

"Then fire her." Enid could not conceal the vehemence in her voice. "She's bad news."

June and Will stared at Enid as if she'd grown warts all over her face.

The door behind her opened and Charlotte, a member of Hector's team, hustled in looking frazzled and out of breath. The young, petite brunette behind her hesitated at the door.

Enid backed against the wall in the crowded room, heartbeat leaping to warp speed. The buggers had found her. A trail of yellow insectoid creatures crawled down Trilly's arms. Heads swiveling in every direction, the tiny pests surveyed their new surroundings. Their constant high-pitched chittering gnawed at Enid's brain.

She glanced at Will and the others. They didn't react. Only she saw the buggers. The infested employee chose then to push her way into the overly full office. She tripped on the carpet. A few of the hitchhiking buggers dropped to the floor. Enid squeezed her body tighter against the wall.

Charlotte gave Trilly a distracted glance then turned to Will. "Hector wants you to send Trilly to another department. We've got—"

"Rats. I know." Will ran his hand through his rumpled hair again.

Trilly looked around, eyes bright with curiosity. "Um, is this normal?"

The silence between the four of them amplified the roaring of Enid's heart. More of the buggers crawled up and down Trilly's arms and shoulders. How could this woman not know she carried destruction with her?

The need to flee swamped Enid. So many in one place.

She inched toward the door as one of the parasites hooked an appendage into the sleeve of Trilly's shirt and swung like an acrobat. A thread pulled loose as it flew toward June's desk, a tiny squeak of triumph, minute but audible to Enid, trebling from its mouth. The heads of the other buggers pivoted at the sound. They swarmed down the thread to the desk.

Easing to the left, Enid inched toward the door. Her act of retreat could draw the buggers' fire. Escape without drawing notice, that's what she needed.

At the door, she checked for any travelers who might have jumped ship on the way into the office. None. She broke for the hallway.

Her muffled bootsteps hurried along the carpet. The last thing Enid heard was Will saying to Charlotte, "No problem, Enid will take her."

She ran out the lobby doors.

In her full-on dash across the parking lot, it hit her—had any of the buggers hitched a ride? Contact with her skin killed them, but heavy cloth or boots could protect them long enough to immigrate elsewhere. Plus, Trilly probably arrived this morning through the same door she'd just exited.

Stopping, she swiped her hands down her body and danced in a circle trying to check her back. Bug-free, she performed a quick scan of the grounds and pavement. The absence of any chittering or yellow critters dropped her rattled nerves down a notch. A full inspection of her bugger-free car inched them lower. It looked like all of the pests went into the plant and stayed there.

Enid hopped into her jet-black Kia Soul. Engine cranked and AC blasting, she gasped for breath. Sweat beaded on her forehead and soaked the underarms of her uniform.

Once her hands downgraded to shaking instead of trembling, she threw the car in reverse and backed out of the space. In five years, she'd never missed a day, never been sick, never took time off except for required shutdowns. The experience—staying at one job for more than one month—had been great, but in the end, the buggers had caught up to her. Took them longer, she had that to be thankful for. That left only one option. Paradise was nice while it lasted. Waving at the plant in the rearview mirror, she sighed. "Hasta la vista, baby."

At the plant exit, Enid rolled to a stop. Go home or leave town? Where had Trilly been before arriving at Henley's? Best get out of town while she could.

Before she could hit the highway, her phone buzzed. The ring-tone, the Beach Boy's "Kokomo," blasted through the speakers. Caller ID identified Will's number.

"No. No, no, no." Enid hit the reject call button. Maybe she should go somewhere like the song suggested—Aruba, Jamaica, Bermuda, Bahama. Well, maybe not Bermuda. No way she wanted to encounter buggers near the Bermuda Triangle. "Probably why all those ships disappear down there."

She turned away from town and floored it, pushing the car as hard as she could, which wasn't fast at all. The farther she drove from Henley's Gaskets, the more the constriction in her chest eased. What to do? What to do? She'd built a life there. Five years without a bugger sighting supported her belief she'd created a protective shield over the place. "So much for that theory."

Ahead, red lights strobed in oncoming traffic. The wail of a siren grew louder. A firetruck blew past her followed by an ambulance.

She wanted to cry but couldn't catch her breath enough to do that. So many of the yellow buggers in one small space, on one little person. Poor kid. Why didn't she feel them? Most people itched even though they couldn't see the fiends.

Two more fire trucks blazed down the road followed by several police cruisers. Four ambulances shot past next. Each one jackrabbited her pulse.

Enid turned off the road and pulled into a deserted convenience store's parking lot. Exhausted, she turned off the engine and laid her head on the steering wheel. "Please no."

Eyes closed, she saw the line of buggers heading for June's desk. Never-a-cruel-word June, who remembered birthdays and greeted everyone with a smile. Will stood behind June's desk, too, in the line of fire. A new dad with a tiny baby finally out of the hospital and a wife who needed him more than ever. Images of the fragile infant covered in yellow buggers gagged her. She heaved the door open and vomited.

Grandpa's words echoed in her ears. "Them buggers will come after you if they get a sniff of what you can do."

The first time she saw a bugger, it was chewing on her best friend, Meggie Anderson. The girl kept scratching at her arm, and her mother kept slapping her hand away. "Stop it. The doctor told you not to scratch."

Meggie's lower lip jutted. Tears welled in her eyes. "It hurts."

Her mother grabbed her by the arm and yanked her into the other room. In a few minutes, the two returned, mittens stretched over Meggie's offending fingers, duct tape securing them from coming off. "Sit and play with Enid," Meggie's mother said, giving her shoulder a nudge. "No more scratching."

Mrs. Anderson plopped down at the table with Enid's mom, shaking her head. "She's been doing this for days. Tore up the other arm. The doctor says there's nothing there. It's just in her head."

"Poor thing." Enid's mother took a sip of coffee.

While Enid watched, Meggie rubbed her arms together over the spot. Three more critters had joined the first one. The sight made her shudder. Unable to understand why no one helped her friend, she swatted one of them.

Pop.

Meggie jumped back, hugging her arm to her. "Don't hit me."

"I'm not." Enid leaned in. "Don't you see them? Bugs."

A howl erupted from Meggie's mouth. Enid clapped her hands over her ears.

"What on earth?" Enid's mom said. "What have you done now, Enid?"

"Nothing Mama." Enid looked into her mother's deep blue eyes, noting the threatening V of displeasure creasing between her brows. "I just tried to knock the bugs off."

"Bugs? What bugs?"

Both women jumped to their feet and stood over the two girls.

"Those bugs." Enid pointed right at them, but the crease in her mother's forehead deepened.

"Enid. Quit telling stories."

"I'm not, Mama. They're right there." She slapped her hand on Meggie's arm, making the girl howl again. As her mother yanked her away, the remaining bugs dropped off. With a subtle pop, each one blinked out of sight.

A grin spreading over her face, she looked up at her mother, expecting praise. Instead, her mother dragged her from the house muttering about never having time to enjoy a simple cup of coffee.

No one believed her but Grandpa. She never told anyone else what she saw or did.

Another line of emergency vehicles flew toward Henley's.

With a deep breath, she stepped around the vomit and walked to the front of her car. Above the thick forest of trees blocking the view of Henley's, smoke billowed into the sky. Bile, hot and gritty, burned her throat.

She banged her hand on the car's hood. This was worse than before.

Her phone buzzed. The screen read Ramone.

With a resigned sigh, she answered it. "Yeah?"

"Where are you?"

"Took a breather."

His voice lightened. "You're not inside?"

"No. What's wrong?" In her head she sang the childhood taunt: *Liar, liar, pants on fire.*

"Explosion in the lab. No one knew where you were. Got to count people. Make sure everyone's out."

She sagged against the car's hood. A strange detachment washed over her. "How bad?"

"Fire in the lab. A few other places."

Through the phone, Enid heard wailing sirens.

"Are you on site?" Ramone now shouted into the phone. "Will's frantic to find you."

"Um." Here came the hard part. The part where she admitted to being a coward, even if she was the only one who knew it. "I had an emergency. Left ten minutes ago. Must've forgot to clock out."

"Oh good." The relief in Ramone's voice made Enid squirm with guilt. "A lot of people got hurt. Some are trapped. Even in the parts not on fire. The doors jammed when the alarms went off. They can't get out."

Eyes closed, Enid tilted her head back. She saw the smiling faces of her team greeting her this morning, calling her Mighty Enid, their friend and good luck charm. How could she abandon them?

"Where's the newbie?"

"Trilly? Good news. She's got emergency responder training. She's trying to help."

Of course, she is. The knot in Enid's belly tightened. She massaged it, staring at the plumes of smoke over the horizon.

"Hang tight. I'll be there."

"I don't know Enid. Just call Will. You probably should stay away."

Yes. She should.

She disconnected, got in the car, and pulled onto the highway, backtracking her earlier flight. "Sorry Grandpa. These people mean too much to me."

A steady stream of cars exited the plant as she turned in the entrance. A highway patrolman manned a barricade. He held up his hand, waited for her stop. "Are you medical?"

Not a local. All of them knew Enid on sight whether she knew them or not.

"Nope. I'm Enid. Boss called me in."

He shook his head. "No admittance. Count yourself lucky."

Just turn around, her brain said, but her heart spoke for her. "Can't. Got a call. I need to get in there and help figure out who's still inside."

The cop lowered his head and stared down at her, unblinking. She stared back, trying not to come across defiant. It wasn't hard; she didn't want to be there.

"Hold on a moment." He stepped away pulling his radio from his shoulder.

She prayed for deliverance. She could say she'd tried. He'd tell her no. She'd blame the cop.

In a few moments, he walked to the barrier, pulled it aside, and waved her through. Stomach flipping over, she pulled forward.

He flagged her to stop. "Check in once you're there. Front lawn. Get a mask."

She nodded, forced her foot to press the accelerator, and drove toward the plant. The fire must be near the hazardous chemicals area. That might work in her favor. Get everyone out and leave the buggers to a fiery death.

Henley's can rebuild.

As she drove down the winding curves of the drive, she caught glimpses of chaos between the thick trees bordering the way. When the building loomed into sight, she eased off the gas. Flames licked the sky above the lab and clean room sections of the plant. The rest of the building looked untouched, but the faces of employees staring up in shock at the flames as they staggered across the lawn, told a different story. A line of ambulances stretched along one side of the main driveway, paramedics tending to the injured. One pulled out of line and sped away, siren and lights screaming its departure.

She parked in the far reaches of the lot and forced her legs into a jog toward the front entrance. The whole time, she kept an eye out for buggers. None. Not surprising. They preferred the thick of destruction, not the outskirts.

Will, a gas mask clamped over his face, stared at a clipboard. She trotted up to him. "Will. I'm here."

Now if that wasn't the most heroic announcement in history.

"Enid, thank God. You disappeared. I thought—" The mask muffled his voice, but she saw him swallow hard. "We couldn't find you."

She nodded but didn't explain. "Ramone said people are trapped. The new girl is helping."

"Trilly? Yeah. She's got training. Good thing, too. It took forever for the firetrucks to get here." He studied the clipboard again and handed her a mask. "Put this on. I need you to—"

"Where?"

"Hang on. I'm looking."

"No. Where are they trapped? Where's Trilly?"

His face relaxed as he studied her. "Don't worry about her. I know you take your team's welfare seriously, but she's a professional."

That one stung. A lot. She cared so much she'd run away. "Where. Is. She?"

With a shrug, Will pointed to the right side of the building, the farthest from the fires. "E&D. Steer clear, ok. I need you to find—"

Enid snugged on the mask and ran.

Will shouted after her, his voice distorted. She could claim she hadn't understood him later.

Engineering and Development had been working on an innovative design. A mega-sized machine expected to change the way Henley's worked. They'd been testing it in the huge, vacant warehouse in the back of the building. A machine with moving parts, pulleys, conveyors, and who knew what else. Everything the buggers needed to rip this place apart.

She closed her mind to that idea and focused on not tripping on the uneven ground.

Coworkers called to her, but she ignored them.

At the door to E&D, another uniform, this one in hazmat gear, stopped her. "No admittance."

"Will sent me."

"Don't know Will. Step back."

"I can stop this." At least she hoped she could.

Behind the face shield, the man frowned. "We've got people trapped in there. No admittance."

She obeyed. Turned away. No one wanted her to help. No one knew she could. She could still run. No one would know.

A deafening crash came from beyond the door. A scream, the voice high-pitched in pain.

Her feet trudged to a reluctant stop. She turned. Studied the door and the guard.

No buggers on the door. A small swarm crawled up the guard's legs, though. An overwhelming urge to cleanse him hit her.

This could get tricky.

The guard faced the building now, so he wouldn't notice her until it was too late.

Here goes my reputation. Enid barreled into his legs. They went down. She slapped at the small swarm infesting his gear. With little pops, they exploded into nothing.

The guard shoved her away and tried to jump to his feet. That was the thing about hazmat suits, though, you couldn't move quickly. And Grandpa made her take martial arts in case buggers ever trapped her.

She bounced to her feet. The guard stumbled to his and lurched toward her.

She threw a side kick at him and sent him flailing to the ground again.

Trilly must be the epicenter. She needed to exterminate these joyriders and get the little troublemaker out of the building. And do it before the terrible, yellow army caused a full-scale, make-national-news disaster.

She trotted to the door and yanked it open.

And stepped into a madhouse.

Yellow coated everything in a throbbing mass of swiveling heads, gnashing teeth, and flashing appendages. The buggers worked in a frenzy, piling at least a foot deep on the exposed parts of the massive machinery. They filled the huge expanse of the room except by the door where Enid stood.

So many. How did they multiply?

From the machine, parts lurched and shook. A high-pitched whine like the sound of a plane taking off echoed against the walls. Robotic arms swung around in haphazard strokes, clumps of yellow bodies flying from them to land on other surfaces.

If they spotted her...

Enid hesitated. No one knew she was here except the guard. She glanced back. He wasn't coming after her, either. *Smart man.* More importantly, the buggers hadn't noticed her.

A metallic screech and groan came from above. Buggers streamed toward the top of the machine. Others followed. The equipment began to rock. Slow at first. More climbed upward. It rocked more. As if someone blew a whistle to summon them, almost every bugger in the huge space raced to join their brethren.

"What are they doing?"

She followed the line of trajectory. If they toppled the machine, it would crash into a large overhead garage door. The door used to be the entrance to the warehouse before they added a lab on the other side. Where people were trapped.

Three firefighters and Trilly struggled to open the large door. Thousands of buggers congregated on the big door, weighing it down. Insectoids clambered over Trilly and the emergency workers.

If the machine fell…

Enid checked the buggers' progress. Except for the ones interfering with the jammed door, thousands more had piled on top of the machine. It teetered, top-heavy with the wriggling, yellow mass.

Time to go!

A few quick steps backward, and she felt behind her for the exit door. A tiny pop made her jump. She spun and quick-scanned the door. The death of some outlying varmint. A vagrant. The door stood clear. She slammed into it and flung herself outside.

The expected run-in with the guard didn't happen. No one was in sight. She should follow his lead and flee, too.

A deafening crash came from inside. The ground shook. The warbling crescendoed.

Over the noise, a voice screamed, "Help!" Others joined in. From inside.

"Bugger!" Enid rolled up her sleeves and pants legs. Contact with her exposed skin killed them. The more exposed, the better. She shuddered at the idea. Jerked the door open and surged into the fray.

The machine lay on its side, still rocking as its conquerors dropped off the edges and headed for more mischief. It had missed the door, the firefighters, and Trilly. The four of them stared in shock at the destruction. She'd seen it before. The confusion from those who could not see their attackers. Go back a few hundred years, and someone would blame a witch for this mess. Probably her.

Rivers of buggers flowed toward the firemen. A new target for mischief.

Enid rushed forward. Fingers splayed, she swiped over surfaces. Pop. Pop. Pop. Hundreds disappeared.

She cut a swathe through the room, slamming into as many covered surfaces as she could. She hoped the massive chaos would keep the creatures from noticing her counterattack. Or the firemen. She had to look deranged.

On the other side of the machine, Trilly and only two firefighters tried to force the huge automatic door up. It pulsated with yellow.

What had happened to the third firefighter?

Enid kicked through the sea of yellow, surrounded by constant popping. A few feet from the door, she stumbled over the passed-out form of the third fireman. Buggers covered him head to toe. She dragged him from the fray, swipe-killing his new friends. Several escaped her touch, retreating toward the masses on the wall.

Leaving the fireman near the exit, Enid turned back to battle. Yellow everywhere, like someone made a huge omelet and slapped it against the wall and floor.

With a deep breath, she ran toward the jammed overhead door, slamming her body against its surface. That hurt, but thousands of buggers blipped out of existence. Others died in her wake. Arms sliding over the door like windshield wipers, she obliterated them. The popping deafened her.

Until a hand grabbed her arm and flung her backward.

She stumbled and came face-to-face with one of the firefighters. The khaki of his protective gear peeked through tiny gaps in the infestation crawling over him. Without a word, she swept his mask clean.

The cleared shield gave her a thrill of triumph. "There."

The firefighter jabbed a finger toward the door. "Out."

She should listen. She was running out of opportunities to flee.

But the space she'd cleared ran yellow again with buggers.

The man returned to the door. They struggled to lift the handles at the bottom, the strain evident even through their gear and infestation. Trilly squatted beside them her hands pressed against the corrugated metal. Probably too weak to really help.

A memory shot into her brain. Something Grandpa told her once. Buggers sprang from one insectoid. Kill the first, you destroy the rest. Somewhere in this mess crawled the original. Her gaze fell on Trilly.

She took a step.

As if they sensed her intention, buggers swarmed between her and the woman.

Others attacked.

Sharp stings on her legs broke her concentration. Pop, pop, pop. *Sacrificial little things.*

She dove at the bugger barrier, a deafening detonation announcing her impact.

The warbling of the mass increased and took on a sinister hiss. A wave lunged toward her.

She ignored the stinging wounds on her legs, took a deep breath, and attacked again. Concussive popping echoed in her ears as thousands more disintegrated.

The firefighters still fought to open the door. Trilly didn't. She'd turned, a snarl on her face. With a scream, she threw herself at Enid.

The blow knocked them to the ground. Enid rolled away, leapt to her feet. Trilly popped up too. The tiny woman shouldn't be a match for her.

Enid barreled into her. Trilly met her head on.

They rolled on the floor. The distinctive popping of buggers dying announced their path. Yellow flashed around them like a crowd of paparazzi on the heels of famous stars.

A platoon of insectoids flowed off Trilly, chomping on Enid's exposed arms and legs. One bite and they evaporated. It stung and burned.

Trilly took advantage of the buggers' counterattack to leap to her feet and back away. She crouched, ready to launch at Enid again.

Enid rose to her feet, swiping her arms down her clothing, killing as she went. She smiled at Trilly. The firemen should have stepped in by now, pulled this crazy woman away, but they still worked at the door, unaware of the true threat.

The chittering grew louder. Trilly raced toward her. Enid charged, twisted, and kneed her in the groin. She bounced back on her toes, waiting for Trilly to go down in agony. She didn't.

Trilly screamed. She lowered her shoulder like a linebacker and rammed into Enid. "Leave my babies alone."

Enid almost went down from the shock of Trilly's words. Her babies? She stumbled backward but stayed on her feet, Trilly falling into her. Arms wrapped around Trilly, the music of buggers winking out made Enid shout in triumph. A new line of defense turned at the sound. They mobbed toward her, their razor-sharp teeth snapping in angry anticipation.

Trilly kicked and screamed, but Enid held tight. She checked the firemen. They still worked on opening the door. Now or never. She tightened her hold on Tilly and hauled her into the melee. Cap-gun-like pops proclaimed her path.

Buggers covered the door and surrounding walls in a gyrating mass. Where was the button to open the massive door? A mountain of yellow swarmed over a raised spot on the wall to the left. She dropped Trilly and ran toward it. A million little heads swiveled to track her. They turned as one and raced her, their teeth snapping. Meggie's chewed up arm flashed in her memory. She bared her teeth and leapt.

Pop. Pop. Pop. The sounds of so many deaths roaring music to her ears.

Pop, pop, pop. It thundered and shook the floor as she, the great exterminator, went to work. Only a few remained. Had she gotten the first one?

Kill it, and the rest die.

The red button peeped out behind some of the more stalwart buggers. She spread her fingers and slammed both hands down on them and the button. "Yah!"

Little incisors stabbed her fingers as she annihilated the creatures. Some hid behind the button's edges, preventing its activation. With a sweep of her fingers around the underside of the knob, she eliminated them and smashed it down, again. Blood seeped from cuts in her hands, leaving a darker red smear on the button.

Hinges squealed. The door groaned upward. Coworkers, her friends, cheered and stumbled into the room. Trilly, smiling and sweet, stood far from Enid, pointing the way—as if people who worked here didn't know where to go.

Except for a stubborn settlement clustered on Trilly's arms and shoulders, the yellow mass had dwindled. As people dashed to freedom, several outliers hopped a ride, choosing the slower ones and the injured.

With a growl, Enid launched herself at Trilly, again. They landed on the floor with a thud. Enid gasped for air.

Trilly kicked at her legs and missed. Then scrabbled for a grasp on Enid's hair and came up empty.

With her army reduced, Trilly didn't appear to know how to fight. Too bad.

Enid shoved her forearm over the woman's throat and pressed down. "Don't. Move."

It might have been the tone of Enid's voice or the pressure on Trilly's neck, but she froze. The temptation to push harder, cut off this woman's breathing forever, trembled on the edge of Enid's mind.

She glanced around. The firefighters were headed their way. She leaned in close before they reached them. "I don't know who you are or where you came from, but you're leaving. Now. Don't come back. This place belongs to me."

A couple of buggers popped into existence on the woman's shoulders. Enid blew on them. They died.

Trilly kicked her feet, trying to gain traction on the floor. "Get off me, you mad loon."

For the second time that day, large hands pulled Enid from her act of heroism.

One of the firefighters assisted Trilly to her feet while the other pinned Enid's arm behind her. Her shoulder and back muscles screeched in resistance.

"Don't know what your problem is lady, but you're going to stop messing with the hero of the day," the man restraining her said. "Without that little miss, a lot of people might be dead."

With a demure smile, Trilly peered up under long eyelashes at the man. "I'm just glad I was here."

Enid snarled but let him push her toward the door. No one understood. Her grandfather had warned her.

She glanced back. Trilly grinned and waved her fingers in a toot-a-loo. A stream of yellow monsters flowed off her feet and toward the exit.

Enid's captor marched her toward the front of the building. The path he took resembled the yellow brick road to Oz. Every time a bugger landed within her reach, she twisted her body to stomp on it. Even if it meant angering her guard. She tried to explain and talk him out of his accusations, but he wasn't local. No surprise considering the number of emergency vehicles responding to the alarm.

Everywhere she stepped the buggers exploded into nothing, but more kept coming. How could she stop Trilly from making them? Especially now. Then it hit her. The world created a balance—one to create, one to destroy.

The firefighter handed her over to a cop, Matt, her neighbor. Without meeting her gaze, Matt cuffed her and led her toward his cruiser. From across the grounds, Will and June raced toward them.

"Matt? What are you doing with Enid?" Will's voice wavered with confusion. Six buggers crawled over the front of his shirt.

"She's your culprit." One of the firefighters strode up to them, body stiff and rigid with anger. "Caught her attacking Trilly."

"She what?" Will stepped back, eyes widening

June pressed her hand against her chest. "Not Enid."

At that point, the guard she'd disabled marched up. "Good. You caught her. I've had men searching for this one everywhere."

"Why?" June's voice leapt an octave higher.

"She attacked me," the guard said.

"Enid?" June shook her head. "This must be a mistake."

Bless her, she still wanted to believe in Mighty Enid.

"It's not what it looks like," Enid called out as Matt shoved her into the backseat of his cruiser. A few buggers roamed around inside. She annihilated them. One remained, taunting her from the other side of the plexiglass divider between the seats.

Outside the car, Will and June gaped while the guard and firefighter regaled them with her exploits. As they spoke, her two coworkers inched away from the car and shifted their gazes from her. Abandoned again by people who had trusted her.

Grandpa's admonishment echoed in her head. "Never tell anyone, my girl. They won't believe you. Them buggers will come after you if they get a sniff of what you can do. You don't want that."

Along her legs and arms, tiny cuts stung, proclaiming her grandfather right.

With no one left to stop them, the galloping yellow disaster enjoyed its victory over Henley's Gaskets. She couldn't tear her gaze away as they multiplied and rumbled over everything and everyone.

Matt climbed in the car and started the engine. He glanced over at Enid. She nodded, unable to fight the manners bred into her since childhood. "Evening Matt." That was the hard part of small towns. Everyone knew everyone's business.

He locked gazes with her for a moment. "Why'd you do it?"

"I didn't."

"You keep telling yourself that." He pulled the car out of the lineup of safety vehicles. He slowed as they came to a clog of news vans in the road. "Your fame awaits you." Reporters raced toward the car followed by assistants carrying video cameras. They swarmed around it just like the buggers, forcing the car to a stop.

"Care to give a statement?" Matt asked.

"No." She leaned her head on the back of the seat. "No one will believe me, anyway."

Someone rapped once on the window. She ignored them. Grandpa had warned her, after all.

The rapping became insistent.

Reluctantly, Enid looked up. Trilly stood close to the window, surrounded by the clamoring reporters, a wide smile on her face. She held up her forefinger. One yellow bugger, at least three times bigger than the others, sat along its length. The first.

With a gentle touch, Tilly stroked her finger along its back. Another bugger popped into existence. She stroked again. Another.

Then the tiny woman turned and pushed through the crowd of news people, a trail of new buggers filling her wake.

Author's Note: I wrote "Buggers" in response to an open call for reluctant hero or anti-hero fantasy short stories. This birthed Enid and her nemesis, the buggers. Unfortunately, my muse took me into the horror side of speculative fiction instead, so it didn't fit the anthology's criteria. I, later, submitted it to another journal where the review committee told me they almost picked it. Where did the buggers come from? I think "Cedar Revenge" a short story that appears in my other short story collection, *Pieces of Her*.

8

1:28 AM

It started with the spider.

Big as my fist, it greeted me from the floor of my daughters' bathroom early one morning. Its body accounted for half its size, the other half long, jagged legs.

I backed out, trying to hide its presence from the girls, and told them to use my bathroom. Praying it didn't disappear on me, I went in search of something large, heavy, and long enough to keep me at a safe distance. One of my boots served the purpose.

Smash! Spider killed.

Fighting the willies, I scraped the corpse onto a stiff piece of paper, dropped it in the toilet, and flushed.

Divorced, this was my job. Protect my children.

I had moved into this apartment in the Atlanta suburbs almost a year before. The new, three-story building sat on a hill, and our first-floor apartment faced the rear of the building. We didn't share the back wall with neighbors. The bathroom shared the wall with the earth.

The next morning, another spider stood sentry in the bathroom. Its legs twitched as if it brandished a sword at me. Shivering with disgust, I sent my oldest for the boot. She returned, but I blocked her view of the invader.

Smash. Flush.

This became my morning ritual: Get dressed, grab the boot, kill the spider, flush, wake my daughters.

One morning two raiders waved their hairy legs at me.

Another morning, the spider hid in the shower. I didn't have time to scrape its body into the toilet that day. When I came home, it was gone. Eaten by its spider friends?

I asked the management to spray. They advised against it. "If we do, the spiders will crawl into your furniture to escape the insecticide."

With a planned move less than a month away, I definitely didn't want anything with eight legs hitching a ride.

We didn't spray.

Spider killing became part of my resume.

A few weeks after the spider invasion began, I woke in the middle of the night to distant music. The faint strains of rock music came from somewhere in the apartment. Stumbling out of bed, I wove through half-packed moving boxes seeking the source. The clock radio between my daughters' beds was lit up, playing the local station. I stabbed at the off button and trudged back to bed.

The next night, rock music crashed my sleep again. I plodded to the girls' room. The clock read the same time as the night before—1:28 AM. My daughters slept through the interruption, oblivious to the late-night concert.

I fiddled with and double-checked the alarm. It wasn't even set, and definitely wouldn't be for 1:28 anyway.

Consumed with packing, spider defense, and the exhaustion of the day, I shrugged it off.

Until the next night.

At 1:28 AM.

Music woke me again. I cursed the radio as I stormed in and turned it off. A different kind of willies shivered along my spine.

Standing between the twin forms of my sleeping daughters, I studied the determined alarm clock, thankful these two weren't aware of this mystery.

With *my* alarm set to go off in a few hours, I headed for bed, checking for monsters all the way. My skin crawled with phantom spiders most of the remaining night. Fitful sleep eventually overtook me.

Friday arrived, the day before the move.

With the children sent off to relatives for the weekend, I finished packing. The clock radio, unplugged and rendered powerless, went into a box. Close to midnight, I collapsed into bed.

A loud, mechanical whirring jolted me awake.

"Why is the vacuum cleaner running?" I grumbled to myself as I trudged after the sound, steering a path through the boxes.

Not to the bedroom.

Not to the hall closet where I stored the vacuum cleaner.

To the kitchen.

The garbage disposal roared, metal grating against metal.

I flicked the switch down.

Silence enveloped me.

The stove clock read 1:28.

I slapped on the kitchen lights, flooding the room with fluorescence. It didn't diffuse the eerie quiet.

Unease swirled along my neck in little prickles. I rubbed at my arms, warding off crawling goose bumps.

The disposal's switch remained in its down position, and I pressed it hard to be sure.

I eyed the sink. The dark hole remained silent.

A scene from a horror movie flashed through my mind. The victim in the movie trapped a rat-sized fly in the garbage disposal and grinded it to smithereens. When he turned the motor off, nothing happened for a few heartbeats, then a cloud of monstrous flies swarmed out of the drain.

It didn't end well.

No swarms, yet.

The room turned colder the longer I stood there.

I hadn't used the disposal today or yesterday, opting for takeout while packing. The empty counters offered no clue to the mystery.

Someone, or something, had to have flipped the switch up.

Mounting terror glued me to the floor. Something *more* than a spider. Chilly fingers of cold ran down my arms and legs. A thick presence settled around me.

A motion off to my side unfroze me. I jumped back. "Whatever you are, stop it. This isn't funny." My words echoed in the apartment, refusing to resound with the bravado I'd hoped for.

I backed out of the kitchen, gaze locked on the switch, half-expecting the presence to thrust it up, fill the room with the whirring of metal blades.

Soft carpet under my feet soothed me. The room's temperature returned to normal. I whirled around and darted through the apartment, flipping on lights as I went. The brightness pushed back the frightening shadows, but the presence in the kitchen played havoc with my sleep-deprived brain.

What was in there?

An uncontrollable drive to understand drew me back. As my feet tread on the vinyl flooring, chill slammed into me like icy hands gripping my arms.

I shot backward, warmth returning as I distanced myself from the unknown menace. Pacing the rest of the apartment, I checked corners and closets over and over, keeping an eye on the kitchen.

The longer I steered clear of the kitchen, the farther the chill seeped into the apartment. I gave it a wider berth.

At 2:30, I reprimanded myself. "This is nonsense. You need your sleep."

In a firm voice, I addressed the presence in the kitchen, "Leave me alone," and stalked to my bedroom.

The lights stayed on.

Sleep did not come. Gaze locked on the bedroom doorway, I reverted to my youth, the covers pulled to my nose, watching for the approach of whatever evil lurked in the kitchen.

As a child, I drove my parents crazy with my fears. Sounds in the night, weird shadows, and creaking floorboards paralyzed me with fright. I recall instances of terror no one else in my family remembers. Like the night someone pounded and shook the outside door to our basement. The width of the hallway, a flimsy door, and stairs separated my bedroom from the danger below. My parents and brother stood in the hallway, arguing over how to deal with the intrusion.

Why am I the only one who remembers?

Another night, I woke to a massive shadow outlined in our bedroom window. It looked like a giant-sized Jinx the cat in the Pixie and Dixie cartoons.

These memories assaulted me.

Questions troubled my soul.

If something could turn on the garbage disposal, what else could it do? After an entire year in this apartment, why did it feel the need to make its presence known tonight?

Maybe it hadn't waited. The spiders?

When told about my eight-legged invaders, one of my friends had chuckled. "They're messengers of the dead. At least that's what my grandma always said."

Who used this property before the huge apartment complex sprawled across the landscape? Visions of rotting corpses scratching free of the earth haunted me. Were the spiders the first to escape the grave?

My brain could not form a logical explanation. Instead, it surfaced a conversation with my mother after I became an adult. Sensing what others don't ran in her family, especially with her mother.

As a child, my grandmother woke to a man standing in front of the hearth in her bedroom, the flames blazing as he warmed his hands by the fire. When she asked the next day, none of the adults had come to her room in the middle of the night. No one had stoked the fire. Fires burned low as the evening wore on, not blazing. None of the men in the house resembled the visitor she saw by the fire, either.

Mom expected I had the ability, too. I could sense the unseen.

Ghosts. Poltergeists. Specters. She knew I felt them as a child but didn't tell me. Instead, I suffered under taunts of "scaredy-cat" from family and friends. Why? Mom knew I couldn't handle knowing the truth as a child. She was right.

Hoping the supernatural power of God would intimidate my haunting spirit, I reached for my Bible. Hours later, I woke at dawn, every light in my apartment still on.

Daytime brought a peace that the night couldn't provide. No menacing presence thickened the air. In its place, a void filled the space. I packed the last-minute items and waited for my friends from church to come help me move.

When they arrived, I rushed to the parking lot, comforted by numbers.

One thing still bothered me, though, so I pulled the wife of our singles minister aside. "Vivian, is there such a thing as a poltergeist?"

To her credit, she didn't laugh or look at me oddly. She gave me her Southern Belle smile and drawled, "No honey, they don't exist."

End of subject. Vivian never asked what prompted my question. I'm sure she believed what she said.

In the new apartment, the children's radio quit providing late-night concerts.

Life moved forward, and the press of unpacking and getting settled distracted me from thoughts of my final night in my former apartment.

Until a few nights after the move, at 1:28 AM, my clock radio made a loud click that woke me.

It repeated this several nights in a row.

I got rid of both clocks.

Author's Note: The middle of the night used to terrify me as a child. What hides unseen in the shadows kept me awake many nights of my childhood.

9

Mistake Number Three

The man standing by the lake studied me like a starved predator lurking in the shallows. His wide-set eyes and intense gaze crawled along my skin. I froze. It had been years, but I couldn't mistake the obvious—definitely one of the Pike brothers.

He started towards me.

I fought the animal instinct to flee and glanced around for protection. One didn't turn their back on a Pike.

No one in sight except this nemesis from a long time ago. I eyed him, noting the changes—a man's body, not a teen's, and a long goatee strand dangling from his jutting chin.

Yep, my plan to restart exercising this morning sounded great from the safety of my parents' vacation cottage. So, here I stood, vulnerable in the early morning hours.

My first mistake.

The fog had been rising over the lake's placid water in a picturesque haze, so I'd opted to run along the shore. The crisp, cool air and the calm before others emerged from their slumber embraced me in welcome. I'd chosen the direction away from the summer homes, though, embarrassed to be seen huffing and puffing at a pathetic pace.

My second mistake.

I hadn't gotten far, stopping, bent over from a sharp stitch in my side.

This flashed through my mind as the man approached, his tongue flicking along his lips.

Which Pike, the bad one or the very bad one? My stomach seized; heart hammered. Indecision still froze me to the spot.

Hesitation guaranteed a mistake.

Three strikes and you're out.

I spun in the other direction and raced toward the cottage and civilization.

A grunt from behind, followed a burst of rapid footfalls pursuing me. Mistake number three?

I kicked my running up a notch. The pounding behind me sped up.

I poured on the adrenaline, body unaware of anything but fear and finding safety.

A quick glance shoved my heart and stomach into my throat, He was closing in. Where to go?

To my right loomed trees, underbrush, and beyond that? It had been years since I'd scampered through those woods with my cousins. We used to swim in a small pond with hidden depths and easy hiding places.

Trees or the lake. Somehow, I didn't think the lake's open expanse provided a hiding place or would deter Pike. I veered into the woods, praying I wouldn't turn my ankle or trip over a root.

Weaving through the heavy-pine-scented trees slowed me down. City living had ruined my agility, just like Mother warned.

I plundered on, the air quiet. Just the sound of my panting, my heart thumping a crazy rhythm in my ears, his heavy treads in pursuit growing fainter. Had he fallen behind?

Then, as my heart eased its drumming, his feet pounded the ground faster. The rasp of his breathing came so close, it burned my neck.

This is how I die.

I rounded a tangled growth of bushes and spotted the large rocks. As a kid, I'd scrambled all over them. He may be fast, but climbing failed him back then. The top had been our safe refuge. But assuming I could make it to the top, I'd be stuck.

Frantic, I tried to remember what the younger me saw from the rock's height.

My brain dredged up the memory of a pond surrounded by a garden. Seen from the highest point of those rocks. With a gardener's shed behind it. Maybe a house. Was it still there? I trotted toward hope.

Wait! Not that way." A gruff voice called. The guy's breathing and steps slowed.

Yeah right, buddy. Like I'm going to fall for that.

Between the trees, I spotted a flicker of light on water. Pushed every muscle into reaching that pond.

Ahead, soft music drifted on the quiet air. People. Safety.

Suddenly, the trees gave way to entwined bushes. Beyond them, a small group of people, dressed in business clothes, mingled by the garden on the other side of the pond. I shoved through the brambles, yanking when thorns pulled back. One last surge, and I dove into the shallows. Body twisting and turning in the embrace of cool water, it returned to the shape I'd forsaken years ago—a sleek otter. My large human clothes flowed behind me as I glided into the depths.

An underwater rock overhang too small for a pike provided a hiding place. Through t he m urky d epths I s aw n othing. Impatience, a need to keep moving, propelled me out from cover.

Darting to the surface, I sniffed the air for the predator. Heavy perfume and the aroma of coffee clouded my nose.

The pike exploded through the brambles, his beady eyes swiveling to me and to the gathering of people on the far side of the pond. Would he break the covenants, too?

A woman screamed. The shocked murmur of voices told me I'd be hearing from the otter council later.

I plunged under the surface and swam for the other shore.

A splash behind me rippled the water. Typical pike, hungry instead of cautious. Wonder what the pike council does with shifters who break the laws?

I scurried onto the shore. My body, unaccustomed to shifting, reclaimed its human form in seconds. Trying to cover my exposed body, I cowered in pain.

A woman screamed again. Voices clamored in surprise.

A polished, and quite expensive, men's dress shoe appeared in my line of sight. Its owner cleared his throat, and a suit coat fell over me.

I gathered it around me and sat up, staring into the eyes of the town's mayor. "Help," I croaked.

The mayor straightened with a frown as the pike soared out of the water and flopped on the ground just a few feet away.

He shifted back; the change more fluid than mine. "Don't. Ever. Do. That. Again." His labored breathing separated each word.

I jumped to my feet, backing away. "What? And just let you eat me? I think not."

The mayor sighed, hands on his hips. His mouth stretched into a thin line. "You two better have a good reason for ruining my morning press conference."

Confused, I turned to the mayor. "This man chased me." I figured if he didn't mention our shapeshifting, I wouldn't either.

Instead, the mayor turned to the pike. "Zack?"

Zack. The bad one at least. Not the very bad.

The large man's jaw jutted out as he rose to his feet.

It struck me he'd kept his clothes when he shifted back. The unfair advantage of a larger size curdled my fear. I pulled the mayor's suit coat tighter around my body.

"Sorry sir," Zack said. "I tried to speak to her and warn her to stay clear, but she ran."

Both of the men stared at me.

"Why'd you run?" the mayor asked.

For a moment, my mouth bobbed like a fish. Then I straightened. "Surely, you know who he is. How dangerous their whole family are to—"

"Whatever is the meaning of this?" A well-dressed, older woman bustled up, a deep line creasing her forehead. "And why is she wearing your coat?" She studied me closer, her eyes widening and the crease evaporating from her forehead. "Are you without clothes?" She glanced toward Zack. "Well, take care of her. Do your job." She stalked away, muttering under her breath. "I miss the old days and better security."

I sidled away from Zack and the mayor, my goal a swift change and the pond.

"Nope." Zack sidestepped in front of me.

He wasn't even wet. How did he manage that? I raised my chin. "Let me go. It's bad enough you forced me to change in public, but I am NOT your next meal."

He and the mayor laughed so hard, the people in the party stopped their chatter. Skin crawling, I fought the urge to turn toward the crowd of witnesses.

"This man," the mayor heaved between chuckles, "is part of my security team. He's no danger to you." He swiped at watering eyes. "Unless you plan to threaten my re-election. Considering your lack of weapons, though—"

Heat flooded my face. I tugged the coat closer and glanced toward the party on the lawn.

As if I didn't exist, they'd returned to their mingling, forgetting the circus sideshow by the pond. Why?

Pulling a bi-fold wallet from his pants pocket, Zack flipped it open. A golden security badge flashed in the morning light. "We stopped scavenging wildlife for food twenty years ago. Where have you been living? Under a rock?"

I felt my face heat up. "Why did you chase me, then?"

"To prevent the media disaster you've created." He repocketed the badge. "Luckily, it looks like the mayor's wife already managed to adjust everyone's memories. And her assistant appears to be handling the film camera issue now."

I studied the small gathering, again. A bespectacled young man of average height and looks held something in front of a news cameraman a few seconds, nodded, and slid away. The man lowered his camera and turned from the pond.

Mind-altering shifters tended to be spiders or cobras. I shivered. Did that mean the mayor was one, too? That would explain his lack of shock when I transformed.

I fought the urge to slump to the ground. They could easily make a snack out of me. I'd never made a mistake number four, before. "Now what?"

"I escort you back to your rental, and we forget this ever happened," Zack answered in a no-nonsense voice.

Not likely.

"Mayor, do you have a phone?" I asked, forcing steel I didn't feel into my voice.

Gaze boring into mine, he shook his head. "My wife holds it during press conferences."

"Here." Zack pulled a plastic bag out of his pants pocket and withdrew a phone. "You can use mine."

Some shifters handled this life so much better than I. Punching in my mother's number, I bit my lip. When she answered, I rushed to speak, praying these two wouldn't grab the phone away. "Mom, I'm being harassed by Zack Pike. If I don't show up in ten minutes, call the police."

"Why wouldn't you show up?" Her voice didn't reveal the anxious concern I anticipated. "Invite Zack to breakfast if he has time. Such a nice man he's grown into."

"A nice—"

"Jeanie, please tell me you didn't do anything stupid."

"I, uh, maybe."

A huge sigh escaped her. "Just come home. I'll handle the apologies."

Defeated and feeling the unfamiliar embarrassment of my youth, I handed the phone to Zack. "Don't suppose you have a change of clothes on you, do you?"

He smirked. "Not your size. No." Then he walked toward the pond and scooped up something near where he'd landed. "But I believe these are yours. They snagged on my fins."

I yanked them from his hands and stalked into the bushes to change.

His chuckle followed me.

Author's Note: I wrote this story in response to a writing prompt in an online writing group. The prompt was: He eyed me like a shark. Originally, I kept the shark, but when I revisited the few paragraphs I'd written, I realized this would not happen at the beach. No. It needed to be by a lake. Then I explored different forest animals with water affinity. I wanted the otter, but I needed a formidable enemy like a shark. That's when I discovered that pike, when desperate, will eat otters. Who knew?

10

Lifelike

"Mom, look." Celia's ten-year-old son Jeremy pointed ahead of them.

Busy monitoring their collie's efforts to do her business, Celia offered a distracted response. "Just a sec."

"But Mom," he whined, "someone's living there."

"Living where?" Celia used the poop bag to scoop up Sheppy's discharge then straightened, her focus on securing the bag without getting anything on herself.

No answer.

"Jeremy?" She turned to locate her wayward son.

Bare feet slapping the road, the impish boy ran toward the old Henley place. The ramshackle house, rumored to be haunted, looked the same except for a few cat and dog statues in the yard. Not to be daunted by the signs of habitation, the boy climbed over the fence where a slat had come loose, hanging from one side. He squatted beside a statue of a Scottish terrier.

"Jeremy, get out of their yard."

Hands running along the statue's back just like he did with Sheppy, the boy ignored her.

The collie pulled her closer, her nose to the ground, and stopped at the edge of the yard. A low whine followed by the rumble of a growl announced her concern.

"Jeremy. Come back here now. We don't know who lives there."

The boy rose to his feet and looked around. "These are cool. They look real."

"Just come on. We need to stay out of the yard. You know the rules."

Trotting back to her, dark brown hair flopping in front of his forehead, Jeremy grinned. "I bet they won't mind. They like animals."

Over the next few weeks, Celia forgot the exchange. Summer had shifted almost overnight to cool Autumn days, and Joey spent his days at school. Most of Sheppy's walks occurred at lunchtime when Celia took a break from answering phones for the local medical offices.

One day in early October, Sheppy chose to do her business within sight of the old Henley place. The yard still looked unkempt, the fence still unrepaired, but smoke curled out of the chimney and an old beat-up Ford pickup rusted in the driveway. "Not exactly improving the neighborhood, are they Shep?" she whispered as she scooped up the collie's latest deposit. Curious, she walked toward the house to get a better look, but the collie whined and pulled back.

"Sheppy, heel." She took two steps forward, but the leash pulled taut. "Sheppy, come."

The dog refused to budge.

"OK. You're right. It's none of my business." She remained in the road a few more minutes, peering toward the yard. Whoever lived there definitely liked statues. Not only had a few more animals—squirrels, rabbits, and deer—joined the domestic pets, there was an adorable one of a young boy squatting as if to pet the rabbit. Everything looked so lifelike, she half-expected the boy to stand or the rabbit to hop away.

Two weeks later, more statues crowded the yard.

Wondering at this new neighbor's curious hobby, Celia returned to home and work. That afternoon, she handled more calls than normal. Autumn and school meant more sickness, so none of this surprised her.

"Whitney Medical, how may I help you?" she answered as the monitor announced which office her current caller wanted.

"Oh, oh, oh." A woman sobbed on the line, her cries close to hysteria.

"Hello? Hello? What's wrong?" These calls weren't common, but enough of them came through in a month that Celia no longer felt alarm when the patient cried instead of speaking at first.

"My baby, oh my baby." The voice rose to a high pitch as the woman continued to wail.

"Is your baby hurt?"

"No, no, no." Sobbing. "I can't . . . I can't . . ."

"I want to help you. Please tell me what's wrong. How old is your baby?"

"She's six." Whimper. "What can I do?"

"Ok. She's six. What's her name?"

Sniffle. "Kinsley. Kinsley Mercer."

"Tell me what's wrong with Kinsley." Celia held her breath and pulled up the screen to contact the EMTs.

A loud whine rang through the headset, so strong, Celia winced. She'd need aspirin after this call.

"Please. I want to help you. Where are you? I'll send an ambulance."

"No, no, no. No use. She's gone."

A chill ran down Celia's arms. "Ms. Mercer, give me the address and I'll send the police and EMTs."

No response, just more sobbing.

"Ms. Mercer, I need your address."

Nothing.

"Is Kinsley there or is she missing?"

While the woman continued to moan and cry, Celia pulled up the Whitney office's patient database and searched for Kinsley Mercer. If she'd been part of the 911 dispatch system like she'd begged her employers, she'd already have an address. If this turned out the way she feared, she'd be sure to take that point up again.

As she sent an instant message to the police, she tried again. "Ms. Mercer? Are you at home? Fifteen Sorrell Lane?" That was just a block from her own home. Should she run over there?

"She's f-f-frozen." The woman keened some more.

Grabbing her phone, Celia raced out the door. At least they'd agreed to her using a cell phone instead of a landline for these calls. Dashing across yards, she tried to get the woman to answer again. "I'm coming to you, Ms. Mercer," she panted. "I live nearby. Police are on the way. Is your door unlocked?"

"Y-y-yes."

Within three minutes, Celia burst through the door of Fifteen Sorrell Lane. "Ms. Mercer?" In the distance, she heard sirens. The house was overly warm, a fire roaring in the fireplace, and a young, red-haired woman knelt beside a child wrapped in a blanket in front of the hearth. She looked up, blue eyes rimmed with red.

"Help her."

Celia dropped to the floor and pulled the blanket back from the child. The skin around her eyes looked pale like her mother's but the rest of her? The rest of her looked frozen in concrete. Life-like just like the statues at the Henley place. As the EMTs raced into the room, the grayish stone-like cast crept closer until only the child's blue eyes stared up at Celia, then they turned to stone, too.

Gone. The child was gone.

Author's Note: Sometimes I can't recall the inspiration for a story. This is one of those times, although the idea sat with me for quite some time before I wrote it.

11

Kaleidoscope

The barista's gaze focused on Heather's hand as she held out the no foam, faux milk, latte. "I love your polish. Where did you find that color?"

"I'm not wearing—" Heather stopped. Her fingernails glowed a rippling shade of aqua. "Oh."

The girl leaned over. "I swear it looks like it's moving."

Heather put the cup down and lifted her hand closer. She didn't get manicures; the few times she had, she'd chipped the polish so many times the salon banned her from touch ups. Yet her nails were the same color as the lady's earrings she'd been admiring moments ago.

Around her, customers chatted, studied their phones, or waited, blank stares hiding their thoughts. She glanced back at her nails. Still aqua. Her heart knocked against her chest so hard she feared others might hear it. As she watched, the nail color twisted and shifted to blood red.

"Whoa," the barista breathed. "You've got to tell me where you got that polish."

"I . . ." The red darkened to the coppery brown of dried blood. *Best to get out of here before something weirder happens.*

Heather beelined for the door. "Sorry. 'Scuse me." She barreled into one woman who didn't see her coming, hot coffee spilling down the woman's cream-colored blouse. Maybe silk.

"Hey!"

"Sorry." Heather ran out the door into the crowded street, glancing over her shoulder. At least no one bent on revenge followed her.

She leaned over and tried to breathe. Hordes of dedicated people swarmed past her, heading to work without noticing the hyperventilating woman in their midst. Her gaze drifted to her hands pressed on her thighs. The nail color fluctuated, flowed. It rippled and disappeared. Normal nails.

"You!" The word exploded behind her as the woman in the cream-colored silk blouse barreled toward her. "This blouse cost two hundred dollars." She shoved an arm toward Heather. She flinched as if slapped.

Coppery red wove along the woman's sleeve where Heather had bumped into her. Not spilled coffee, like she'd thought. It was the same color of her nails—or at least the color they'd been at the time.

"I—" Hot bile burned her throat. Heather clapped a hand over her mouth and weaved like a drunk on a Saturday night bender toward a curbside trashcan. Half-digested breakfast spewed onto the sidewalk before she could get to the can. Now, people noticed; noses wrinkled as they edged away from her.

"Some people." A gaggle of high heel clacking women muttered to each other, not bothering to hide their disgust as they swept by.

The woman in the blouse threw her hands in the air. "A drunk? Great. You ruined my favorite blouse."

The barista rushed out of the coffee shop and pushed past the angry woman who spun toward her. "Someone will pay for this. My husband's a lawyer." She stormed away.

The barista frowned at her retreating back, then turned to Heather with the latte she'd left on the counter. "Are you ok?" She touched Heather's arm. "Come. There's a bench over here. Out of the way."

Like a child, she followed the young woman to the bench and slumped down on it.

"Put your head down and breathe through your nose." Belinda, or so her nametag proclaimed, patted Heather's back and stood sentry over her, brows drawn in concern.

This street was in a nicer part of town, so the deep breathing didn't trigger any more nausea. A florist's sidewalk display a few doors down perfumed the air. Funny, she'd never noticed the fragrances extending this far before.

When she sat up, Belinda handed her a bottle of water. "Sip. Don't swallow. Just rinse. I have a cup for you to spit into."

Obeying, she drank, swished, and spit into the cardboard cup held before her. Belinda smiled. She had a piercing right above her lip. The tiny stone glinted in the sunlight in a prism of color. Never one for facial piercings, Heather found the glistening stone oddly comforting as she sucked in air.

"How does it do that?" Belinda pointed at Heather's nails again. They'd shifted to a crystalline shade, just like the gem winking at her above Belinda's lip.

"I don't know." Heather turned her gaze from the girl, hoping the color might fade again.

"There it goes again!" The excitement in Belinda's voice jerked Heather's attention back to her treacherous hands. Her nails now whirled in the same shades as the crocus display outside the florist shop—purple and yellow.

"Seriously," the barista said, "you have to tell me where you got this polish."

"Nowhere." Heather closed her eyes. Maybe she was dreaming. She'd spent too long breathing in paint fumes preparing for today's presentation. That had to be it.

"Nowh—" Belinda's voice bordered on annoyance. "I mean I get it's special, but seriously?"

Should she explain? It was a dream after all.

"Look. I took a chance leaving the counter to help you. And that woman . . . The least you could do is tell me."

It wasn't like she knew where the colors came from. She opened one eye enough to peek at her nails. The floral shades faded, and her own boring, unpolished nails were returning. "I don't know what you mean. I'm not wearing any polish." She held up her unadorned hand.

"Right." Belinda's sharp, sarcastic laugh croaked to sudden silence. "Wait. You had polish. Beautiful polish. Where—"

Still a bit unsteady, Heather pushed up from the bench. "Listen, I appreciate you helping me when I got nauseous in there. No clue why, but thanks. Maybe someone else had the polish?"

Guilt over her denial flamed heat into her cheeks, but Heather ignored it. She took the spit cup, wobbled over to the trashcan dodging the pool of vomit, and tossed the cup in the can. When she turned back, the barista's brown eyes squinted at her.

"Look, Belinda, I don't know what you think you saw, but—"

"There." Belinda pointed at Heather's hands. "It's back."

A deep brown, like Belinda's eyes, spread across them like a rising tide.

Heather did the only thing she could think to do. She turned and quick-walked away, disappearing into the crowds of people.

Navigating a sidewalk full of office workers without looking at colors was impossible. She could close her eyes and run into people or hide her nails until she got someplace safe. She opted for safety. Her apartment.

As she pushed through the crowds, she called work. "Hey Chloe, it's me, Heather. Look, I'm not feeling well."

"We have the Sensation Paints presentation in half an hour." That was Chloe, straight to business.

"Yeah, I know. But I don't think I—"

"What'd ya do? Throw up?" Chloe chuckled.

"Well, actually—"

"I bet it's nerves. Look, I get it. I remember my first big client. You must be here. I've built you up as the top color specialist in the state, if not the country. No way I'm telling them you're out sick. Whatever it is, stop at the pharmacy and grab something. Just get here."

The call ended before Heather could object.

With a loud sigh, Heather about-faced. A man pulled up short. "Whoa. Use a turn signal or something." He smiled, friendly lines crinkling around the bluest eyes she'd ever seen.

"Sorry." She held up her phone. "Work."

"Deadline?"

"Yeah." She glanced down at her phone. Her nails adjusted to the same blue as the guy's eyes, complete with a dark iris in the center of each one staring back at her. Clutching her phone to her chest, she stepped to the side. "Gotta go."

Giving everyone on the sidewalk a wide berth, Heather hurried back the way she'd come, toward the office of Artisanal Advertising. Her nails faded back to normal as she walked.

What would she do if they continued to shift like this? And how in the world did her touch change the color of that woman's blouse? As she passed the florist's, the bright flowers taunted her. She glanced down. Sure enough, the purple and yellow swirls had returned. If she touched something, would she paint it purple and yellow?

A jean-clad guy bouncing his head to silent music on his ear-buds thrust a neon green flyer toward her. She took it, turning away quickly. A wave of purple and yellow rolled across the sheet, obliterating the green. A frantic giggle escaped her lips.

"This is not good." She ran her hand through her hair, then paused. If the color transferred to the paper, it might work on hair, too. She moved out of the oncoming crowd, tapped her phone, and activated the camera. When she hit the reverse camera mode, her face appeared. A thick strand of purple and yellow wove down her hair in the exact path she'd run her hand. Just great. This presentation was lost before it began if she didn't find a solution, and fast.

A bell jangled as Heather pushed through the door of a clothing store two doors down from the florist. She struck a straight path to the closest salesperson. "Gloves. I need gloves."

"Gloves?" The petite brunette laid down the pair of yellow shorts she'd been folding and blinked at her. "It's not the right season."

"Do you have any?"

"Hmm." She tapped a finger on her bright pink lips. The woman's nails matched her lips.

Heather didn't dare look at her own hands but couldn't stop herself. Yep. They'd shifted to pink. She curled her fingers into her palms. "I'm desperate. Anything will do."

"We have a clearance table. You could try that." Waving a pink-nailed hand toward a table in the back corner, the woman picked up the shorts again. Together, the colors reminded Heather of her grandmother's strawberry and lemon sherbet.

"Thanks."

The clearance table held an assortment of dark-colored sweaters and pants too heavy for spring temperatures. Beneath a pair of navy sweatpants protruded the finger of a black glove. Perfect. Black absorbed all colors, so maybe her strange new touch couldn't affect the gloves.

The soft leather slid over her fingers, hiding the nails, now the shade of Grandmother's sherbet. It might be too warm for gloves, but at least she could conceal this catastrophe. Once the presentation was over, she'd beg Chloe to give her the rest of the day off. And do what? No clue, but right now the gloves appeared to be working.

* * *

"Why are you wearing gloves?" Chloe demanded when Heather entered the conference room.

Before she could answer, Clark, the receptionist, stuck his head in the door. "The execs from Sensation Paints are here. You ready?"

Eyebrow arched in Heather's direction, Chloe shook her head. "Give us five."

"Got it."

"What did you do to your hair?"

"My hair?" If the streaks of color remained, would that be a good or bad thing? This was an ad presentation for a paint company, after all.

"Go run a brush through it, real quick. I'll keep the client entertained."

The restroom mirror reflected a very disheveled woman but no purple and yellow swirls. Running leather gloves through it made things worse, the strands clinging to the gloves with static. For the moment, she had the restroom to herself, so off they came. Holding her breath, she studied her nails. No new color.

Sagging with relief, she rubbed her nails. Nothing changed. "Why are you doing this to me?" She chewed her lip, a habit she'd conquered in her early teen years. The countertop felt cool as she pressed her palms on it and leaned toward the mirror. Her phone buzzed in her pocket, and she fished it out.

From Chloe: *Hurry up!*

A quick swipe through her hair with a pale blue comb bled the same color over the tips of her fingers. On went the gloves again before she could accidentally change the color scheme in the ladies' room to pale blue. "It's like Midas," Heather grumbled. "We know how that ended for him."

A chill scampered up her neck. Would she be stuck this way? Never able to look at colors or touch anything again? Color was her life. She reveled in finding the right blend of shades for each client, the ones fitted to their product and personality. This was why Chloe gave her the Sensation Paints account. Everyone knew she saw color differently.

"Get a grip, girl." Heather turned on the cold water, yanked a paper towel out of the dispenser, and ran it under the water, keeping the fingertips of her gloves as dry as possible. When she draped it over the back of her neck, the rocks tumbling in her stomach settled. Some.

A deep breath. And another. She tossed the towel, forced a smile at her reflection, then headed for the conference room.

A few raised eyebrows greeted her gloved handshakes, but no one commented. That was the good thing about dealing with high-level professionals. It reflected badly on you to call attention to a random oddity early in the game. Before today, she'd only met the

CEO, Samuel Blanding, a trim and suntanned man in his fifties known for his impatience. Sensation Paint's CFO and head of R&D, otherwise known as Blanding's twenty-something daughter and son, Marla and Mason, settled around the conference table.

Artisanal Advertising's red and white animated logo, a pen sketching an apple, danced on the large LED screen mounted on the far end of the room.

After fumbling to separate the pages of her notes, Heather took a deep breath and dove straight into the script she'd spent hours perfecting. "Samuel, Marla, Mason, thank you for joining us today. With Artisanal's love of color and your line of new and vibrant paints, I believe our vision for Sensation's future will take us on a magical journey." She clicked to advance the slide, and an image of a yellow brick path appeared.

Marla and Mason frowned, but Samuel leaned back, nodding.

"The yellow brick road helped Dorothy and her friends pursue their dreams."

Click. The slide animated to a red road, then a green one, then a blue one. "However, let's face it. The yellow brick road wasn't a barrel of monkeys."

A few small chuckles from Marla and Samuel, but Mason remained stoic. It wasn't the response she'd hoped for. Heather reached for a glass of water and sipped, eyeing the three. In the back of the room, Chloe bug-eyed at her, waving her hand in a "get moving" gesture.

She tried to put the glass down, but it slipped from the glove, tipped over, and flooded the table. Water streamed toward Samuel.

"Oh, oh, oh!" Grabbing some napkins from a credenza, Heather rushed to stop the flow. She sopped at the water, but the gloves made the job impossible.

"Give me that." Mr. Blanding grabbed the napkins. "Why don't you take those ridiculous gloves off? It must be eighty degrees outside."

A raised eyebrow and chin jerk from Chloe reinforced this command.

"Of course," Heather whispered. She peeled the gloves off, breath held. Unpolished, blunt nails. Clean and professional. She turned away to grab a waste basket for the wet napkins and breathed a sigh of relief. Grabbing some more napkins, thankfully plain white, she assisted in the cleanup. The last thing she needed was color shifting nails right under the man's nose.

Spill handled, Heather returned the wastebasket to its corner of the room and turned back to face the Blandings. A strand of hair fell over her eyes, and she shoved it out of the way. The sudden intake of breath from the others told her all she needed to know. She looked down. Her nails shone bright white. That would mean . . . She turned toward the mirror over the credenza. Yes. She had a skunk stripe running from her forehead toward the crown of her head.

Mason recovered first. "Amazing." He sat up, eyes gleaming.

Chloe and Marla tilted their heads in confusion.

Mr. Blanding shoved back from the table and rose from his seat. "What are you trying to do?" His face flushed a blotchy red. "Rub our faces in the fact that White's is pummeling us in the housing market?"

"What? No." Heather rushed forward, her gaze locked on the man.

Another gasp.

Biting her lip, Heather looked down. The same blotchy redness in Mr. Blanding's face bloomed across her nails.

Marla jumped to her feet. "I don't know what kind of parlor trick you're pulling, but that's not funny." She scowled at her brother. "Are you just going to sit there?"

The young man didn't acknowledge his sister, his blue-eyed gaze fastened on Heather. It unnerved her, and she ran her hand through her hair again. He grinned.

"I've seen enough." Mr. Blanding jerked his head toward the door. "Marla, Mason, let's go."

Father and daughter marched for the door, but Mason remained seated.

"Mason." It came out as a command, the kind a parent uses on a willful child.

"But her nails are blue now. So is her hair." The young man shook his head. "You can leave, but our business *is* color. This is just what we need."

The other two huffed out. Chloe shot a dagger look at Heather then raced after them.

"I appreciate your enthusiasm, but you don't need to stay." Heather slumped into a chair and dropped her face into her hands.

"Whoa, careful." He leaned forward. "No driving with your eyes closed."

"No driv—" With all the confusion, she hadn't recognized him. Heather studied her nails. Yep. They'd turned blue, the color of his eyes. At least they hadn't picked up the black iris to stare back at her this time. "I ran into you this morning."

"Yep. Ran into would be correct." He moved to a chair next to her. "I thought I was seeing things this morning, but—" He reached for her hand. "May I?"

She hesitated, but he'd already seen.

He tapped her pointer finger. The blue painted his fingertip.

"How did you—?" She swallowed and blinked several times.

"You've tested the paint samples I sent over?" Mason leaned toward her.

She nodded.

"The one called Kaleidoscope?"

"No. A delivery man bumped my desk and knocked that sample over."

The whole mishap had confused her. The paint spilled in a clear puddle, but as she mopped it up, it became opaque, shifting from one color to another and another. The experience prompted her to create the color-shifting path on the slide.

"When?" Mason's voice turned insistent. He gripped her hand hard and wouldn't let her pull it away.

"Three days ago."

"Much faster." A distant look settled over his face.

While Mason appeared distracted, she jerked her hand out of his and jumped to her feet. "You drugged me?"

Unease itched down her spine when Mason pointed to one of the company's signature red folders and tapped it. His fingertip, not his nail, turned red. He stretched across the table to the open folder his father had left behind and tapped the first page of the proposal. Red seeped out of his finger and onto the page.

Torn between desire to sprint from the room and curiosity, Heather shifted back another step, but only one. Curiosity won.

"I have to touch the color, but you—" he raised his gaze to hers "—you just have to see it?"

Heather held out her hands to reveal the nails had turned red. "Or think of it." The sherbet shade from earlier wobbled into view. "You *did* drug me."

"No—well, not really. I promise it won't harm you. It's all natural."

"So's belladonna."

He roared with laughter. "It fades. You'll be fine. Your Midas touch will be gone." Then he turned a brilliant smile toward her. It lit up his face like the sun. "We're going to make so much money!"

She felt the blood drain from her face, but her nails ignored her fears. They glowed a bright, blinding yellow.

Author's Note: I wrote this story in response to an anthology's call for stories filled with magical and magnificent feats of wonder. I was stumped for weeks on what to write because I didn't want to go the obvious route of circus, carnival, or superhero. This idea came to me only a few days before the submission deadline. It was chosen and appeared in the 2024 JordanCon anthology: *A Magnificent Display of Marvelous Wonders.* This story is a Finalist in the 2025 Imadjinn Awards. The winner will be announced a few months after the publication of THE NATURE OF THE BEAST.

Acknowledgements

I've been writing stories all my life. In fact, before I could read or write, I dictated them to my Aunt Vivian--or so she tells me.

This compilation includes short stories written for a variety of reasons including contest entries, newsletter subscribers, and intriguing writing prompts.

Two of the stories aren't fully fiction, but I'm not going to tell you which ones. See if you can guess!

Only three of the stories have been previously published anywhere, and they have undergone some edits and revisions since then. The originals appeared in other anthologies:

- "A Good Trade" first appeared under the title "Lifesource" in Vol 1, No. 6 of Stupefying Stories published by Rampant Loon Press in 2012.
- "Whippoorwill Calling" first appeared in Vol. 7 of *The Petigru Review* published by South Carolina Writers' Workshop in 2013.
- "Kaleidoscope" first appeared in *A Magnificent Display of Marvelous Wonders* published by JordanCon in 2024.

Thank you to my readers, subscribers, and beta readers for wandering into the world of my imagination and sharing the journey with me and the characters hanging out in my head.

Barbara V. Evers hails from the mysterious Dark Corner of South Carolina where she crafts fantasy stories with strong women matriarchies and clever animals. She is the award-winning author of THE WATCHERS OF MONIAH epic fantasy trilogy (The Watchers of Moniah, The Watchers in Exile, The Watchers at War) as well as numerous published short stories and essays. A two-time winner of the Imadjinn Best Fantasy Novel, she's won many writing awards over the years including a Pushcart Prize nomination. Her short stories and essays have appeared in multiple issues of *The Petigru Review,* multiple issues of *moonShine review, Child of My Child, Stupefying Stories, A Magnificent Display of Marvelous Wonders,* and her own short story collection, *Pieces of Her: Being a Woman is Not for the Faint of Heart.* She's currently working on an urban mountain fantasy series, The Matriarch Enchanter, and several other projects.

Barbara is a supporter and advocate for giraffe conservation and seeks to educate others about the giraffe's silent extinction. As an advocate, Barbara donates a portion of her royalties to support the work of The Giraffe Conservation Foundation.

When she's not writing, Barbara uses her degrees in Zoology and Communication to conduct training workshops for businesses. Maybe she really can speak to animals!

The rest of the time, Barbara can be found herding her husband, two grandchildren who live with her, and her rescue dog, Roxy (but don't tell them).

Also By Barbara V. Evers

The Watchers of Moniah Trilogy
The Watchers of Moniah
The Watchers in Exile
The Watchers at War

Short Story Collections
Pieces of Her: Being a Woman Is Not For the Faint of Heart

Other Works
Giraffing Around (forthcoming)

Join the Watchers' Tribe newsletter at https://www.barbaravevers.com. As a welcome gift, you'll receive a short story from the world of Moniah. Subscribers, also, receive early notice on new releases, access to subscriber-only contests, and updates on appearances and giraffe news.

Turn the page to read the beginning of *The Watchers of Moniah!*

Excerpt from
The Watchers of Moniah

PROLOGUE

Queen Chiora of Moniah leaned back on her throne, her gaze steady on the traitor, Maligon. The sight of her once truest friend tightened the knot in her stomach. The gathered nobles hushed as he strode past them, head held high, escorted by two women of the queen's Watchers. The heat in the air lay thick as a blanket. The silence matched it. Chiora resisted the urge to shift in her seat as sweat pooled inside her uniform, the leathers chosen over ceremonial dress to remind him she was a soldier, not just a figurehead.

Sunlight poured into the open courtyard and radiated across the landowners' formal robes of glimmer cloth, creating a rainbow of iridescent color around them. Normally, she enjoyed the play of the sunlight on their clothing, but today she couldn't. Today, they waited to witness the sentencing of the man who dared bring destruction to the kingdoms.

The Watchers and Maligon came to a stop below Chiora's Seat of Authority. He wore the plain clothes of a prisoner but still stood tall and well-muscled, his dark hair tied back in a fighter's tail. His black eyes once caressed her in love, but now they radiated hatred so pure it shimmered in the air.

"Maligon," Queen Chiora spoke, her voice firm and strong, "you betrayed me. And so you betrayed us all. And for what? Power you didn't need."

Maligon's black eyes didn't blink. He sneered at her. His injured hand twitched. She watched it with dispassionate interest. He'd never wield a sword again, a satisfying bit of knowledge even if he was about to die.

She took a focused breath, centering her mind and soul. "I sentence you to wear the oxen head into the desert."

A low murmur of approval hummed through the onlookers.

Maligon continued to stare venom at her as she gestured to the Watchers. "Take him from my sight."

The two Watchers, dressed in the tanned leather tunics and leggings of Chiora's all-female guard, escorted Maligon from the hall. He walked between the tall soldiers, head still held high.

Chiora drew a deep breath, the tension in her muscles easing as the air spread into her chest and throughout her body. She took another breath, and another. With each controlled inhalation, she drew her focus inward, preparing to bear witness as her soldiers carried out Maligon's sentence outside the walls of her fortress. The sentence would finish him. The heat, even this far from the desert bordering her lands, baked the air.

As her breathing settled into a steady rhythm, she sent a tendril of thought into the telepathic link with Ju'latti, her royal giraffe. Tension slid from her neck and shoulders as the noble beast embraced the connection. Through this link, Chiora looked through the animal's eyes and saw a throng of tribal villagers gathered outside the walls of the fortress. They stood near the horses where the soldiers led Maligon, but not too close. She couldn't blame them after the devastation the traitor and his followers wreaked on their lands.

Two Watchers lashed Maligon to the back of a donkey, securing the bindings so neither traitor nor beast could dislodge the man. Then they handed a large skin bucket to a squad of First Soldiers, the male branch of Moniah's military. At the edge of the desert, the soldiers would remove a water-soaked oxen head from the bucket and secure it over Maligon's.

Chiora squinted at the sky. The sun, now a short distance above the horizon, promised a scorching day. Just before it reached its pinnacle, the First Soldiers would place the suffocating weight of the oxen head over Maligon's. A few hours later, the soldiers would stab the donkey's rump, driving it farther into the desert. In the heat, the wet oxen head would dry and conform to Maligon. Suffocation would kill him long before the donkey collapsed from exhaustion.

And if he survived? Chiora shook her head. No one had survived this sentence in hundreds of years.

The thought of this torturous death repulsed her, but Maligon made his choice when he defied Moniah and her allied kingdoms of Elwar, Belwyn, and Teletia. He didn't deserve the pity that rose in her throat.

As the soldiers and Maligon disappeared beyond the fortress walls, Chiora released the remaining tension in her shoulders and let the giraffe's gentling influence wash over her. Only Ju'latti truly knew her thoughts and feelings on this ominous day, and in the way of their long relationship, the animal sought to comfort her by cutting off the sharing of sight and focusing on the soothing sounds of the large, life-giving fountains in the Great Hall.

The queen focused on the gentle bubbling and ignored the stream of sweat trickling between her shoulder blades. "Send in the champions."

The assemblage shouted their approval as two foreigners walked forward to accept the accolades they deserved. The men's lighter coloring no longer startled Chiora unlike the day she and a squad of Watchers found them at the bottom of a muddy cliff. The man on the right, Micah, saved her life during the war with Maligon. Her gaze ran over his tall, lithe build in appreciation. Light hair, bleached white from the sun, glowed against his Monian-kissed suntan like bones on the prairie. Clear blue eyes gazed at her with startling familiarity, stuttering the pulse in her neck.

She drew another calming breath as his companion knelt before her. Unlike Micah, this man's fair skin had blistered and burned in the harsh sun of their land, a point that favored the reward she would grant him.

Micah maintained his focus on her and nodded in acknowledgement before kneeling. Chiora breathed deeper to suppress the shiver of excitement prompted by his forthright behavior.

"Our dear champions." Her low-pitched voice echoed throughout the huge open hall. She thanked the Creator that it came out strong and clear, with no hint of the emotions tumbling her soul. "Your journey from beyond the northern mountains came at a fortuitous time. Your courage in the face of our recent struggles brought peace to our lands. As reward, the kingdoms have decided to grant you titles and property." She turned to Micah's companion. "Donel, you will be known as Sir Donel and receive land as a vassal to Queen Roassa of Elwar."

A glimmer of a smile ghosted his face. She suspected his pleasure stemmed from admiration for Roassa rather than the title and cooler climate. Her sister queen shared this interest and had suggested his placement in Elwar rather than Moniah.

Whereas, Chiora could not stop thinking about the other man before her. Micah.

She stood and approached him, placing her hand on his shoulder in the formal greeting reserved for one of her subjects. "As for you, Micah—"

As her fingers settled on his rough, leather vest, the bond with Ju'latti surged into her mind in a flash of light. She gasped, closing her eyes. An image appeared. Micah stood by her side. Between them stood a young girl, her skin a blending of Chiora's amber-colored skin and Micah's pale complexion. The child's hair was twisted into a Watcher's braid the shades of a lion's mane. In the image, the girl walked away from her parents. With each step, they faded from view, first Chiora, and then Micah. The girl continued to walk forward, alone.

The landscape around the child changed, first the flat plains of Moniah, then the mountains and forests of Elwar. With each step, the girl matured. She halted at the top of a hill, now a young woman dressed in leathers, a quiver of arrows strung over her back, a sword at her side. The shadow of a man emerged from the forests and stood beside her. A divided path lay before them, one route blocked by a monstrous blazing fire, the other by a wall taller than the eye could see. The young woman raised her head, blue eyes blazing, and stepped forward, aiming for the point where the two paths merged together in a wall of conflagration. The man's shadow followed.

Chiora bent over, gasping for air, as the vision faded. Two Teachers of the Faith rushed to her side, their green robes swaying in their urgency to support their queen, but Chiora remained upright, her fingers digging into Micah's shoulder. He rose to steady her, a look of concern in his eyes. She gazed back at him, the warmth of his touch flooding her veins.

The Creator had not only sent her a champion to help defeat Maligon, he had sent her a partner. They would make a strong child together, an heir to Moniah's Seat of Authority. A child who would face insurmountable struggles.

CHAPTER 1

Moniah, 20 Years Later

Adana believed deep within her soul that her actions today could save her mother. The familiarity of the dirt-packed ground of the archery arena and the blazing Monian sun beating down on her did little to distract her from the haze of incense hovering over the fortress. Incense that proclaimed the illness of her mother, Queen Chiora of Moniah.

Tiny rivulets of sweat trickled down the contour of Adana's back. She focused on the damp track as it ran beneath her leathers. Anything to pull her mind from the weight of grief hanging over her and the kingdom.

She couldn't lose her mother. Not yet. Not when she still needed her guidance, teaching, and even scolding when she forgot her training as a soldier and acted like a princess.

The work of a soldier came first. Not the princess. And definitely not her future as the queen. Even the laws of the land knew this. Three years until she could rule at eighteen. Too soon.

She glanced at Montee, the Watcher assigned to work with her today. Montee hadn't moved, standing still, arms hanging by her side, attention focused on the young princess. Adana expected her to say something. She had taken too long to make this shot, but Montee waited.

As did everyone, today. Waited for their queen to die.

If she met this challenge, passed this test, would the Creator reward her and heal her mother? Give her back the time she needed, the parent she craved?

She drew an arrow and nocked it to her bow.

Nine arrows in a straight line pierced the scarred target wall in the distance. A significant feat and cause for jubilation for most trainees, but she didn't rejoice. Not yet. Not until she fired this last shaft. Sent true to its mark, she prayed it would prove her worth to the Creator and save her mother. She didn't care about the promotion in the ranks of the Watchers, the fact that no fifteen-year-old had ever passed this test. She only needed to please the Creator.

She inhaled. The noxious fumes of the incense, thick and cloying, settled around her. She wanted to run, to shake her head, to escape the reminder, but instead she raised her bow.

A nudge at her mind disturbed her focus. Am'brosia, her royal giraffe, offering assistance with this last shot. The animal had hovered in the background of her thoughts all morning, seeking to connect, to comfort Adana, but she'd closed her internal eye and ignored the contact, unwilling to risk the joining of their vision. Afraid Am'brosia might show her the reality of her mother's illness.

Focus.

She set her stance.

The white sun beat down. Beads of sweat pooled beneath her Watcher's braid. Adana inhaled and closed her eyes, seeking a center within her breathing, extending her mind and ability. Each inhalation spread through her chest, down her arms and legs, giving life to her focus. She breathed again. Again. Again.

Heat, sweat, and incense faded from existence. Adana envisioned the target.

She let loose the arrow.

Thunk.

The shot penetrated the wall at a perfect interval from the other nine arrows. Most Watchers released their control and shouted with joy after succeeding in this trial, but Adana dropped to her knees in thanks.

Heart pounding, she fought the urge to weep in relief. The Creator would save her mother. Save them all. And save her from this grief.

Montee studied the target, her green eyes squinting in the bright sun, then turned toward Adana. "Good," she said. That brief word rarely crossed Montee's lips.

With the heightened awareness brought on by her focused breathing, Adana found her gaze drawn to the deep lines etched within the golden skin around Montee's eyes. The premature wrinkles combined with a warrior's height and hard, muscular stature, proclaimed the Watcher as a member of the elite female branch of Moniah's military. Some day this soldier, and all the women honored to be trained as Watchers, would serve Adana. Not today, she reminded herself as she rose to her feet, waiting for further instruction. They still served her mother, as it should be.

"Aim for the spot between the fifth and sixth arrow," Montee said.

Adana nodded but wondered at the new challenge. Did Montee think she could do it? Or did she seek to remind her of the humble nature of her position?

No matter. She would succeed. A year of practice, that's what it took to pass the straight line of arrows test, but she could do anything now that the Creator would heal her mother.

Heart racing in anticipation, she set her stance.

"But first connect to Am'brosia."

Adana faltered at Montee's words. Dread ran down her spine like cold water. Lowering her bow, she stared at Montee.

What if Am'brosia chose to show her what she'd avoided all morning, Ju'latti, her mother's giraffe, suffering from the same illness? Clear proof of how deep the connection between the royal and giraffe went.

Doubt crept into her mind. What if the Creator wasn't pleased? What if he demanded more?

"Please, not today…"

Montee narrowed her gaze, silencing Adana's objection.

Adana faced the target, took a breath, and drew an arrow. She took another breath and raised her bow. Only royals sensed the presence of the bond. If she appeared to connect, Montee wouldn't know she hadn't.

"Adana." Montee's warning tone invaded her thoughts. "You will be the only one linked to a giraffe in battle. You must master this."

What small motion gave her away, hinted at her disobedience? With another Watcher, her defiance might have worked. But not with an attentive and experienced Watcher like Montee.

She whispered a brief prayer, "Please Creator, heal Mammetta." Then she inhaled. As she exhaled, she sent a tendril of thought toward the giraffe and gasped at the strength Am'brosia used as she seized the connection. Not the gentle embrace Adana had grown accustomed to.

Discover the rest of the story: